FLASHBACKS!

(tall tales & cliff hangers)

Jeannette DesBoine

FLASHBACKS!

Copyright © 2016 by Jeannette DesBoine
OCO Independent Publishing
El Sobrante, CA 94803
oco2@sbcglobal.net

Geometrics: Jeannette DesBoine
Caricature of author: John McKenzie - McNary, TX

Library of Congress Control Number: 2016906665
CreateSpace Independent Pub. Platform, North Charleston, SC

ISBN 13: 978-1514279038
ISBN 10: 1514279037

Printed in Charleston, SC - USA

FLASHBACKS!

FLASHBACKS!

Flashbacks!

PREVIOUSLY PUBLISHED

Thanks to
El Paso Community College
Senior Adult Program
Eastside Center Creative Writing Class
(Judy Vasquez)
for prior publication
in the following anthologies:

"Down Senior Street"

Spring 2015

Best Buddies
The Writer
Sum of Its Parts

"A Thousand Fridays"

Winter 2015

Fireworks
Wheels
Memory is a Muscle
Squeaky
Rhinoceros

ACKNOWLEDGEMENTS

KUDOS to:

James C. Marshall, George W. Bernard III, James Eugene Marshall, Melissa Bellamy, Dolly A. Dixon, Loretta Steens, Cheryl Bennett-Scales, Andrea Weber, Larrie D. Green, Larry A. Chrispyn, David Levi, William Cummings, TheArthur Wright, Judy Vasquez & the EPCC Eastside Center creative writing class, Donna Snyder & the Tumblewords Project (El Paso, TX); to my creative writing students, to family, friends, fellow writers, teachers (especially Sylvie Carberry); and the many others not mentioned here today, but thought of every day. Thanks for being my inspiration, my encouragement, my sounding board, my winding stem, my mainspring, and my basic rock and roll.

And, extra special appreciation to my second set of eyes, Judith Van Herik, Professor Emerita, Penn State University, author of "Freud on Femininity and Faith." Peace, joy and blessings.

- JD

DEDICATED TO

Akilah

Desmond

Taveis

&

A. J.

(my grandchildren)

FLASHBACKS!

is a collection of narratives
born of non-threatening techniques involved in free-writing;
(*serendipitous approaches to discovery of new ideas and liberation of thought*)
its principal purpose being to entertain.

All characters are fictitious.
Resemblance to any individual(s), living or dead,
is purely coincidental
and a stroke of absolute genius!

The format includes stories and diaries for the young at heart
as well as outtakes from
U-Finish-It (UFI[jd]) files used in specific teaching techniques.

Welcome to Flashbacks!

FOREWORD

ON WRITING

ready or not

censored or uncensored

words spread on pages

like jam on bread

like mustard on a bun

like toast

crisp and crumbling

waiting to be devoured

by cauliflower dreams

and rooms for rent

ONE

MEMORANDUM

To:	Mr. Francis Ulysses Peyor
From:	I. M. Sams, Chief Operations Officer
	National Eternal Revenue Department
Subject:	THE POOR TAX
Date:	Today

In answer to your recent tax inquiry, Mr. Peyor, the rule is: "less income - more tax." And just as the rule indicates, sir, the less money you make, the more taxes you pay. However, your terminology identifying the phenomenon as a "Poor Tax" is misnomer. Your government has no tax structure which can be directly identified as a "Poor Tax."

While it may seem that you are paying more than your fair share of taxes, Mr. Peyor, let me assure you that this is not the case. According to our audits, sir, your percentages are not only accurate, but they are just. In addition (and in case you may be unaware) there are methods by which you may relieve yourself and improve your situation. Basically, Mr. Peyor, you simply increase your income and your financial burden decreases accordingly. Increased income translates in devices known as loopholes. These loopholes are also known as credits. The more money you make, the more credits you earn. Make enough money *{and the right friends}* and your credits grow into exemptions. Eventually, these exemptions work FOR you, Mr. Peyor. In essence, sir, the more money you make, the greater your reward. Yes, your government actually rewards you for having money! With enough money *{and the right friends}* you will eventually achieve our most coveted TAX-FREE status!

Meanwhile, Citizen Peyor, as you work toward your new and more rewarding income tax bracket, you must be penalized for your current posturing. You are not trying hard enough Mr. Peyor; therefore, stringent modifications and limitations must be attached to and imposed upon your account. It is as simple as this Mr. Peyor: POVERTY COSTS! Yes, poverty costs and therefore you must pay, and pay dearly, I regret to say. Your government recognizes that this is only a temporary condition, however, and we of the National Eternal Revenue Department (NERD) know that you possess more determination than you currently exhibit. We are certain (no, positive) that you will successfully strategize and realize significant augmentation to your present income. As we maintain that confidence, Mr. Peyor, please be advised that if you fail (for any reason) to execute this increase in your income we will be forced to watch you belly up, file bankruptcy, and join the rank and file homeless. Our hands are tied on this one, Mr. Peyor. That ball is in your court. You control your own options, Mr. Peyor, but as far as options are concerned, please know that your revenue department has found rank and file homelessness nonviable. We vehemently oppose this course of action.

Further, in regard to your query concerning your resident children... Well, Mr. Peyor, your resident children are no longer eligible children, therefore, they no longer qualify as allowable deductions. The rationale for this originated and is indexed in STATUTES AND NATIONAL LAWS ON TAXATION (VOLUME: 666, SECTION: 8). Children are indeed blessings, Citizen Peyor (and deductible) but our procreation tax-break is transitory, and not a long-term fix. Always read the fine print, Citizen Peyor. This is of extreme importance. Pay particular attention to our "age-out" clause, sir. Children are only children until they reach the age of eighteen and become independent and self-supporting tax payers in their own right.

As for the economic issues that you raised, sir, please don't concern yourself with [1] outsourcing; [2] high unemployment rates; [3] inflation; [4] soaring real estate costs; [5] failing economic trends; or [6] living indoors. All of the negative reports that you have heard on these issues are merely political hype and social propaganda designed to throw our enemies off track as we territorialize the globe. {Global territorialization is currently one of our country's major top-secret strategies, Friend Peyor; *but you didn't hear that from me!*}

Also, sir, you solicited suggestions in possible solution to your personal problems. Well, as I see it, Mr. Peyor, two or three of those minimum wage jobs is a good start for you. You can do it, sir! And regarding your lack of sleep; well, according to the latest scientific medical research, sleep is (and has always been) overrated. And your health...? Well, yes, you must stay healthy so that you can continue to work. That is your responsibility. Our advice is that you keep some aspirin around. Take one every day. Doctors and hospitals are perks that you must work up to, but we know you will do it, Citizen Peyor. Why, just look at how much you presently contribute to the system. At the rate you are going, it won't be long for you.

Finally, in answer to your question about shelter and such, you just keep saving up and soon you will have a place of your own. And transportation! And maybe even a gas card! You have so much to look forward to, Citizen Peyor, and we are always here should you need our hand. Our voicemail system is at your disposal twenty-four hours a day, seven days a week. Call us any time. And, please note that our interest and penalty rates are remarkably low. A mere 29 to 40 percent, compounded hourly. And no, that is not sharking, Citizen Peyor. It is perfectly legal. We would not cheat you, Citizen! We are not crooks!

Well, keep the faith, Mr. Peyor, and please give our most eager regards to all the little Peyor's.

In conclusion, sir, I trust that I have answered all your questions, Citizen Peyor, and that you better understand your obligations to your nation.

We thank you, Mr. Peyor, for the opportunity to serve you.

Yours until you are tax-free *(like me)*,

I.M. Sams

Isaac Meriwether Sams
Commander & Chief of Operations
National Eternal Revenue Department (N.E.R.D.)

ecc: F.U. Peyor

THE WRITER

"Who's going to tell our story?"

"What do you mean?"

"Who is telling the story, Debra? You? Me? A third party? Who?

"I don't know. What difference does it make?"

"It makes all the difference, moron. It's point-of-view."

"What???"

"Listen, doe-doe, if I tell the story from my point-of-view, you will come across as a mental midget. Excuse you!!"

"Oh, yeah? And what if I tell the story? What will you be?"

"You tell me, genius!"

"You'll be a real witch -- spelled with a capital B. You'll be pushy and shallow and ignorant and self-indulgent and egotistical and, above all, not such a good-looking person."

"Oh! Ugly am I?"

"Of all the traits mentioned you only latch onto ugly? You are so vain, Constance! I can't believe you!"

"Right! I'm vain and you're stupid! Who's going to tell the story? Let's get back on track, okay genius. First, what is our story? What is our story about? What's the plot?"

"Plot?"

"Plot, Einstein. Plot. What's the story about?"

"It's about us, dear heart. About you and me."

"You and me what?! DUH!!! Who the heck are you anyway?

"Oh, Geez! I don't believe you, Constance! I'm your sister, dumb-dumb! Remember me? Debra! The smart one! You are some piece of work."

"Yes, I **am** some piece of work. And this piece of work doesn't care about being any part - of any story - that includes you - and has no plot."

"Listen!"

"I'm through listening! You're writing this dip-stick story. Dip your ink pen in your own spit and write away! You tell your story. I'm going out. I'm the one with a life! You're the hermit locked away in the fairy tales of your imaginary mind. You tell this so-called story, genius. I've got a date. Good-bye, Hemingway!"

"You make me sick, Constance! I hate you! Go on! Get out! GO! I don't need you anyway!"   Hmmm....let's see now...

> *Dear Diary:*
> *It was the best and worst of times for twins like my sister and me. Her whispers lay heavy on my heart like stones rolling over hostile horizons...*

THE RED BAG

I've been bugging management for months and still there is no screen on my kitchen window. I'm in a second-floor studio flat with one window. I need air, but not mosquitoes and flies. If I look on the bright side though, that missing screen translates to a perfect vantage point for people-watching. And, trust me, I am devoted to people-watching. Some days I sit in that window for hours. I'll sit for days if my money is funny and I can't afford to go out! The long edge of the kitchen table is shoved against the wall and my two chairs are situated at either end of the table. The chair under the window is my station. I can stick my head out the window and still use the table while I watch - undetected. I see them, but they don't see me. I'm on the second floor! Who looks up nowadays? Right. Nobody! I've got the perfect set-up.

Last night was rough, and since I couldn't sleep, I got up early, made coffee, took my station, turned the chair toward the open window, rested my elbows on the ledge, stuck my head out and proceeded to watch the day progress as I sipped the mean, black brew I call coffee. I popped some bread in the toaster, made a light toast and added a final few dabs of grape jelly scraped from the bottom of the functionally empty jar.

Just before six a.m. a tall (6'5" or 6'6"), graceful figure strolls up 23rd Street. The glossy red bag draped over his shoulder caught my eye, held my attention, and filled my head with all sorts of questions.

What kind of a man carries a purse? Or a bag looking like a ladies purse? Is that patent leather? And red! Why red? What's up with this? Why would he be carrying that? Where did he get it? What's in it? What is he all about? Maybe it's a specimen! I dismiss the questions for want of answers. Maybe it's his lunch. I nibble at my toast.

This guy holds a high-head (like mama used to like) and he takes his own sweet time heading toward the bus stop. He walks like time is his child. I don't think it's deliberate; it's just an unconscious strut. Beautiful.

What a nice day. The sky is clear, the weather a bit crisp, but at least it's not raining. The tail end of his windbreaker flaps like wings on his breezy manner. His stride and the stretch of his long limbs communicate the type of confidence that would permit such a giant of a man to carry a purse, a red patent-leather purse at that; be it lunch, specimen, or whatever.

*

POPPOPPOP! Sudden explosions of gunfire spin me around! I snatch my head out of the window, drop to my knees, crouch down, sneak a careful peek over the windowsill, canvas the street, spot the source of the sound and watch a tricked-out white Chevy whip around the corner and peel down E. 14th Street towards San Leandro. I look to the right and the tall man is face down on the pavement. Blood fans out across the back of his windbreaker, pools under his body, and puddles under his chin. I back away from the window, straighten up, jam my feet into my shoes, throw on my coat, grab my cell phone and dial 911 as I run down the back stairs. Oakland Police Department is 'on the way' by the time I get across the street to the tall man. He's still breathing.

I don't know how many shots I heard, but I can see that three met their mark. One in the neck, one in the right shoulder, and one through the left lung area. All the shots entered from the back. I let him know that I am there. "Take it easy. I called the police. They're coming. And an ambulance. Stay still." His eyes are glassing. I don't know if he understands me. I don't even know if he hears me. I squeeze his hand. No response.

Two motorists stop their cars and get out. The younger driver has blankets in his back seat. He lays a receiving blanket under the tall mans' cheek to get his head off the concrete then covers him with a child-size comforter. Thank God for good Samaritans. Sirens are coming from the direction of Park Street and Highland Hospital. I hope they're coming for us. The man is still breathing. I keep a firm hold on his hand as I sit on the concrete and whisper in his ear. It doesn't matter whether he understands me or not at this point, I just want him to hear me and hold on. I want him to stay awake and keep breathing. The Samaritans keep pressure on the wounds, trying to contain the bleeding. A crowd gathers as people from my building and surrounding areas come to see if they can help. I hear one of my neighbors talking to police dispatch again: "... *please hurry!*"

The first cruiser arrives. Uniforms begin crowd-control. Seconds later, plain-clothes arrive and move toward the fallen man. AAA Ambulance parks and begins to prep the victim. "Back! Move back!" Police begin to clear spectators, dismissing folks, and for some reason I tell OPD that I am this guys' wife. Why? I don't know, except for a feeling and a voice in my head that said "Do not leave this guy alone! Go with him! Go!" And I hear myself say: "my husband."

Triple-A is deep in its job. Everything happens really fast. In all the chaos, focus switches from crowd-control to interrogation. Bystanders are questioned. Notes are taken and contact information recorded for future use. I will be questioned later at the hospital. The paramedics secure the I.V. They hook my 'husband' to monitors and start life-saving procedures as I climb into the back of the ambulance next to my fictitious mate, holding his hand and praying in his ear. We race to Highland's Emergency Room with sirens blaring. Highland is only a few blocks away so he's in E.R. and on to surgery in record time. I get as far as the waiting room. Even this early in the morning Highland is crowded. Somebody actually offers me a cup of coffee! I take it and sit with the coffee cup until Admitting summons me to sign some forms on behalf of my spouse. *My spouse. . .*

> *{Oh Lord! How will I admit that I am not this man's wife? "Someone must have misunderstood me! No, I don't know him! Well, I must have been hysterical!" How will I tell them that I know nothing about the man in the windbreaker, and that my only connection to him is this red bag? I tighten my grip on the strap.}*

"His breathing is weak, but he is still hanging on." The admitting nurse starts her update but the charge nurse interrupts for yet another *code blue*. "Sorry, we can't talk to you right now!" I am dismissed. I return to my seat to sit and wait. The morning drags on and on. I sit so long my legs go numb. I get up and walk around to revive my circulatory system. I check in at the front desk again but Reception has no further information on the surgery. I pace and wait. I stand up. I sit down. One hour turns to two. I squirm. Three hours. I stand. I pace. I sit. I zone out.

**

A nurse is shaking me and calling me Mrs. Miller. I stare at her for a moment and am about to tell her that she has the wrong person when I realize that there's been a shift change. "Dorthea," I say. "I'm Dorthea." The night-shift must have used his wallet and I.D. to enter information into data-base. Somebody must have mentioned *'the wife'* and pointed me out. And somebody else assumed. We are a society of assumers. The day-shift nurse wants to let me know that my husband "is still in surgery, but, it shouldn't be too much longer." The doctor will speak with me 'as soon as it's over.' I thank her. She walks away. I am Mrs. Miller. At least until the surgeon shows up.

I'm hungry. Shards of curiosity stab at my hunger pangs. I still have custody of the red bag, and now, along with custody comes need-to-know. I unzip the bag, look inside, and find food: a sandwich, a bag of chips and a soda. Lunch! It really is a lunch bag! (Maybe it was a gag-gift from a co-worker, or from some sadistic family member.) I stick my hand in the red patent-leather bag, extract the sandwich, unwrap it and take a bite. He won't need it.

CODE THREE! STAT!

GUNSHOT WOUNDS! WHEELING IN TWO!

DR. RUSSELL TO ER SEVEN! DR. STANLEY RUSSELL - ER SEVEN - CODE THREE!

I barely finish the last bite of ham and cheese before the P.A. system blasts the silence wide open. Emergency staff dashes around like the crew on that TV show 'House'. Like everybody else, I try to see what all the commotion is about. A white Chevrolet, pulled up in the 'ambulance only' entrance, prods me alert and lifts me to my feet. Faint smoke from the exhaust pipe says the motor is still running while the incoming gunshot victims are placed on gurneys and wheeled into E.R. My God! This is *my* white Chevy! This is the Chevy that shot Mr. Miller. There's no doubt in my mind. I'd know those spinners and that tricked-out air-brush job anywhere. I need the plate number! I've got to get the plate number! I rush to the door, read the plate and repeat the number in my head while I run to the Reception desk for something to write with. "I need a pen and paper! Please hurry! It's an emergency." AJL675H. AJL675H. AJL675H. I keep mouthing the number so I won't forget. A thick woman in strained spandex hands me a pencil and some scratch paper. I scribble the license plate number from my head to the paper, drop her pencil on the counter, dig my cell phone out of my coat pocket and dial 911. Before OPD can answer I spot an officer in the waiting room. I charge at him and drag him out of hearing range of the crowd. I guess I look pretty desperate to BLUE because he lets me pull him to the side without taking any defensive stance. "That car!" The words come out in spurts. "That's the car that shot a man this morning. He's still in surgery. Inside! That's the same car! I saw the whole thing!" I gasp air. I don't know if I'm making any sense, but the cop listens as I rush through my story. No sooner than I get my words out he zips to Reception and starts talking to the charge nurse. I'm right beside him. He makes notes on his pad, radios the station for backup, and orders me to take a seat in the waiting room, "out of the way." The driver of the white Chevy is still answering questions at Admitting. I try to slow down my breathing. Inhale, hold, release! Inhale, hold for 10, release. I have got to calm down.

The driver of the white Chevy continues checking the gunshot victims into the hospital. "No", she does not know anything about the shooting. "No", she doesn't know what happened. Relationship to victims: mother. My mouth flies open. My pulse races so fast my head throbs and those shiny little diamond halos float on my peripheral vision. "Jones," she states her name. I listen and stare. I keep blinking, trying to get my focus right. Did I take my blood pressure meds this morning?

Mother Jones' victims are being prepped for surgery. One is a severe head wound. I can't hear what the other is. OPD detains *mother* for questioning. The Chevy is impounded for evidence. The pager is so loud I can't hear...

"MRS. MILLER: WHITE COURTESY TELEPHONE. DORTHEA MILLER: WHITE COURTESY TELEPHONE PLEASE. DORTHEA MILLER!"

"Oh my god, they're paging me!"   I grab my red bag and run.

CATCHING THE BUS

Long story short, I sashay my narrow behind up to the bus stop thinking: *'Good, nobody here. No crowd.'* I hope I haven't missed the bus. I concentrate on what I've got to do and on the time. It's already 12:15 and I've got to get to the Credit Union and make it back to work by 1:00 (give or take a minute or so). I'm standing on the corner of 14th and Webster, downtown Oakland, a two-block walk from the transfer stop, about a foot behind the corner bench. These new shoes are killing me! But I'm in a hurry. No time for sitting. Gotta keep these shoes stretched.

I'm wrapped up in business, time, and my aching feet, so at first I don't notice anything unusual. But then I hear someone talking and I see a figure sitting alone on the edge of the bench, talking to no one in particular, or so I think.

I return to my world. 'Where is that bus?' I look up the street, hoping to see the bus coming, and down at my watch to check the time. I shift my weight from my right foot to my left. I wince and stare down at my swelling ankles. All of a sudden I hear screaming. *'What the...?'* The noise startles me. No, it scares me. Well, to be perfectly honest, it freaks me out! I take the blood-curdling screams like a fist in the face. I am jabbed into instant awareness. I hear another scream, this time even more severe, and I actually jump backwards. Intense screaming is coming from the figure on the bench. Now I really take notice. The figure is female and fifty-ish. Her look says homeless. "Bag lady" would be current terminology, but this is no time for linguistic accuracy. A bag lady, screaming like a banshee, has captured my full attention. (My friend Charlie Williams pops into my head. Charlie likes lecturing me on how I need to learn to pay closer attention to my surroundings.) Well, my instantly alert mind quickly conjures up a million mental pictures. Mixed and mangled images explode in my head. Images like hyena, homeless hag, Bag Lady from Bellevue.

Suddenly I flash on Ronald Regan who, in his tenure as governor emptied-out and closed-down all the orphanages and mental institutions in the state of California. Many of his suddenly exiled victims simply froze to death on the streets that first winter of eviction. Well, this is Ronnie Reagan's fault, I reason. This is his legacy! His casualties continue to this day. This is what he should always be remembered for. Here on this corner, on this day, is another one of Ronnie's victims.

The legacy sweeps cobwebs from my mind. I weigh this situation and my options. Danger is my situation and fear is the sensation that surrounds all options. *(I'm paying close attention to my surroundings now, Charlie! Believe me!)*

I finally recognize some of the words in the shrill screaming. "Get away from my bench," is the command. "Get yo' nasty ass away from my bench." Frenzied movement accompanies the warning. My mind clicks. Danger! The phrase "yo' nasty ass" knocks on an already jangled nerve! Those words linger on frightened air, attach to my newly acquired awareness banks and paralyze my limbs. I see a light! It registers: 'this witch is crazy.' I sense another *click* and I become my own computer. My brain is processing *(click/click);* my heart joins in *(thump/thump);* and I've got my own symphony going *(click/click/thump/thump).*

By now my throbbing feet are riveted to a spot about a foot or two behind the bench. Instinct rides in on adrenalin. I look for safe haven. My head swivels left and I see what happened to the usual bus crowd. The bus stop is in front of a stream of open and operational businesses. Huddled discreetly in a doorway adjacent to the action is a little passel of people who came before me. 'Smarter than me' slides through my mind. They avoid eye contact. They actually avert their eyes from me to blank spots on the sidewalk under their feet. 'No help there,' I decide. 'She already ran them off and has them cringing in the doorway of the mom and pop gift shop...the one with the oriental flare...the one that sits just outside the real China Town.... You know the place!' *(click)*

The hag starts to swing a metal cart through the air. My mind registers an 'Oh, my God,' while it notes that this cart is no ordinary shopping cart but a wire carrier on wheels like the kind used for travel and for up-scale shopping sprees. I am ready to duck if she swings that thing near me. The carrier appears heavy and hard to maneuver. *(click)* Her belongings are neatly folded and precisely stacked to the top of this state-of-the-art carrier. *(click)* She grabs the handle with both hands, takes an awkward lunge in my direction and swings that thing in wide arches at my head. As she gains momentum, the carrier gains height. Higher, higher and closer, closer with each swing! *(click/click/thump)* Some of her things fall out. *(thump/thump/click)*

Don't ask me why I am processing details about the uniqueness of a carrier and its neatly folded contents because I have no idea! She is fanatically aggressive *(click)* and my mind is processing irrelevant details *(click)* along with serious warning signals. *(thump/click/thump)*

Fear makes your mind race. And the things to which *this* mind is racing are out of the realm of all control. Another light flashes! The flash confounds me. I remember thinking: 'She has a collapsible steel cage, on rollers, in excellent to new condition.' 'She is filthy. Her hair is matted and nasty and yet, she has no body odor. How can that be?' *(a cymbal crashes!)* 'Don't break the

31

skin! AIDS! Not in the teeth! Avoid all contact!' I hear my knuckles crack against themselves.

Right about now I rest assured that this woman is certifiably insane and is as filthy as she is nuts! I am frozen. I cannot will myself to move. Fight or flight? Where are my options? I am riveted to the concrete. And she is still swinging! And still screaming! She yanks the cart again and it breaks loose from her grip. The fancy carrier flies through the air, crashes to the ground and bounces on the sidewalk, spilling more of its contents. Still shouting obscenities, she rights the cart, gathers her fallen possessions, jerks her way back to the bench, flops down (probably exhausted) and begins to fold and restack her items. I stare in disbelief.

I hear my symphony. It picks up speed. *(thump/thump/click)*

The message transported from her head to mine translates to invasion of space. I invaded her territory. I entered her home uninvited. I am an uninvited guest. I am two steps behind the bench. Her bench! I cannot move. There's no place to go. The bus! The bus! I do not speak but I hear Kenny Rogers: *"You got to know when to hold 'em, know when to fold 'em, know when to walk away, know when to run..."* I shut down the sound. The bus has come.

When the bus stops, I skirt carefully around our girl, not taking my eyes off her, and get on board. I give the driver my transfer and hasten to an empty seat by a window facing the action. I look out the window. The passengers from the mom and pop doorway make their way to the bus also. I survey the little group as they climb out of their hideout: one Black woman who stood guard (or was left standing guard) at the front of the pack; four nondescript white-boy business types tucked tightly in behind *sister girl*; and a couple of dark-haired females with almond eyes who lurked

32

behind all the rest, forming the rear echelon. All of them probably out to take care of some personal business on their lunch hour, just like me.

I am annoyed with them. I am angry that they did not bother to alert me to a potentially dangerous situation when I passed their little huddle. Even though I didn't notice *them* at the time, they, most assuredly, witnessed my approach and arrival. Why didn't they say something? They should have issued a warning. That would have been the neighborly thing to do. I mentally curse them and call them all kinds of trash! Peering through the window, I notice that **she** has gathered her possessions and placed her things back into her righted carrier. She is motionless. Her eyes are dark. She is so still... Still, as if nothing at all has happened.

On the return trip I notice that the woman is no longer there. She and her possessions are gone. I wonder if the merchants called the police and had her removed. Maybe the police took her to hospital. Maybe they took her to jail. Maybe she got cleaned up and fed and an available shelter was found somewhere for her. My mind gives her a name. She becomes Ms. Hannah! *Mzz* Hannah!

When I had reason to visit the credit union again that next week, I approached that particular bus stop with caution. I certainly would not be caught unaware a second time. The bench was empty. I could see that from a block away. She wasn't there. I took a mental note of my emotions. I was relieved. I was genuinely happy that this woman was not at her bench. Not home!

Fran, a good friend of mine, was on the return bus that day. She and I have been fast friends since the seventies when we were both relatively new County hires. We talk like sisters. I told her the bizarre tale and she asked if I had been afraid in the incident. My answer came like an out-of-body explosion: "ABSOLUTELY! And believe you me I'm glad she wasn't at home when I passed by there again." I was shaken just talking about it.

Maybe it was a look on my face or something in the tone of my voice as I re-enacted the event, I didn't dwell on it, but at any rate, Fran, and a stranger sitting a few seats behind us, burst out laughing. I looked over my shoulder, gave the tuned-in sister a weak nod along with a look to let her know that I definitely was not being funny. The bus neared my stop. I pulled the cord and rang the bell. End of conversation. I left the bus with my Ms. Hannah still on my mind.

I think about Hannah to this day. I actually worry about her. I hope she is still alive. I hope she is safe and warm. I hope she has enough to eat and a nice place to stay.

On the other side of the coin, I sometimes wonder if this incident was for real, or a game? And if it was a game, what kind of game? Her cart was too fancy. Her belongings folded and arranged to the point of obsession. She should have reeked from the look of her, but didn't. Was she for real or a plant? Sometimes I imagine her to have been undercover vice squad. Was she really that homeless hag? That hyena? That bag lady from Bellevue? One of Reagan's minions, or a mole?

That was years ago. The bus no longer stops at that corner and I like to imagine that Ms. Hannah shut that corner down. Maybe it was a major drug deal corner and Ms. Hannah was really there working the day shift. *'Detective Hannah! OPD! Vice! Undercover! You're under arrest. You have the right to remain silent.'*

But bus routes change over time. It probably had nothing to

do with my Ms. Hannah. Perhaps my Ms. Hannah found herself a better bench. Or maybe a shady place in the park. Or maybe she found herself a shelter; or a real home (if she were really homeless and not a cop).

Is it possible for fear to shut down olfactory glands?

Can terror totally and absolutely turn off the sense of smell?

Totally?

Absolutely?

I know a little bit about the tragedy of homelessness, and when I see people living on the street I think about Ms. Hannah. I also think of the conditions of homelessness, and of the lives (past and present) of the homeless and reflect that there, but by the grace of God, go I and millions more of America's masses; the working-poor classes who live just one paycheck away from a personal bench.

I tell Ms. Hannah not to give up. It's a mental exercise.

"Don't give up Ms. Hannah. God has prepared your destination."

And I pray, knowing full well that there, but by the grace of God, go I.

Jeannette DesBoine

TWO

THE INVITATION

"Church!? When you say church, that don't mean I gotta go hang out with YOU all day long, and let a lot of other weird people all up in my personal business do it? 'Cause if that's what you mean, Lola, then I pass.
Humph!
Yeah! Right!
And good day to you too, Lola Mae!"

I told it to her just like that. In that vernacular! In words she could not possibly misunderstand. I wanted there to be no possibility of misinterpretation in my answer to her demeaning invitation. Church indeed! I wanted her to *feel* me, so I gave it to her *ebonic* style. She walked away in a huff, commenting under her breath about my lineage and my sanity.

Normally, I speak to people using all the diplomacy and tact drummed into me as a child, but this reaction just came up and out. Later, in reflecting on the incident and wondering why I "went there" with Lola, a very old picture filled my mind. I remember the age of innocence. I am in church on Sunday morning wishing they would hurry up and get to the part where we get to go home. The choir is singing. I always liked the singing but never cared too much about the rest of it.

I'm in Shiloh Baptist Church. I hate hats, but at Shiloh every female head wears a hat unless that head is serving on the usher board or singing in the choir. I guess it was times and tradition, but I had one of those mothers who made you go to church. No excuses. Not only did you go to church, but you wore a hat, like a "proper lady."

The part of church that I really hated was the sermon. The yelling and screaming got on my nerves, and the words did not make sense. Being Catholic, my father didn't go to our church. He, my brother, and my cousin all went to mass at St. Josephs. Whenever they took me with them I found their services, well, quiet.

Religiously, the men went one way, the women another, but my father always quizzed me on what I had learned at our services each Sunday. I was terribly confused after sitting through the "Holy Mackerel Lamb of God" sermon so I asked my dad about it. I waited a long time for the laughter to subside before he told me that he was sure the preacher must have said: "Holy Immaculate Lamb of God." Well, I heard the whole sermon that day, and the preacher never said that! Never! But I felt better and wiser after my dad's explanation; especially when he stopped laughing, and the tears stopped rolling down his cheeks, and he assured me that he was not laughing at *me*.

But, getting back to Lola Mae, the service she reminded me of was a long one, and, if I remember correctly, it was exceptionally hot in the church. I can't remember what the screaming was about that day, but as always, the sermon was followed by the collection, the recognition of visitors, and the benediction. I always looked forward to the benediction. (I love the sound of the word benediction. Loved it then. Love it now.)

The choir always sang "God's Giving" at collection time. Collection was a call for money, tithes, and financial support for the preacher who had no job. Mom said I was always wanting the preacher to get a job so I could take my nickels and dimes to the candy store instead of putting them in the collection plate. "If you had two nickels," she told me, "you would only give the preacher one, and keep the other one for yourself." What she didn't know was that if she wasn't looking I kept both my nickels (and all my dimes, if I had any.) Times were hard for little kids!

"Giving!" The choir was never better than when they sang this song. They sang it every Sunday so they had plenty of practice. I believe that this song, as it was used at our church, was designed to impose guilt feelings in the hearts of the congregation and thereby separate them from their hard-earned dollar bills.

I listened to the music as four ushers in pristine white uniforms and short white gloves came forward, waited for the deacons to bless the collection plates, positioned themselves at each side of the pews and circulated two collection plates, row by row, from the pulpit to the exit doors. This took a while, and the choir kept right on singing until every person in the church had been given the opportunity to dig deep into their guilty little hearts and strained pocketbooks to try to beat God's giving.

The congregation sang along with the choir: *"You can't beat God's giving, no matter how you try. The more you give, the more He'll give to you. Just keep on giving, because, it's really true... It's true that yoooouu can't beat Gods'givinNGGGGG...no matter how-ow you try."*

I remember the old woman in the white dress as if it were yesterday. I can see the black flowers plastered on the white fabric like badges; and the stiff, see-through collar that made the cotton dress look hot and itchy. She wore a white hat trimmed in the same stiff fabric as the collar of the dress. That skull-cap hat covered her entire head and accentuated the countless crevices in her dark face and short neck. She wore short white cotton gloves. I don't know if her hair was gray or purple, but I can tell you that she wore that Sunday hat like a "proper lady."

41

I remember her most as the old woman who, when the collection plate was passed, picked up each tithing envelope, fondled and squeezed each one in search of the fullest, fattest and heftiest. When she found the best one (which took a noticeable bit of time) she quickly palmed it and held it in her gloved hand as she passed the plate on to the next person. When the plate was no longer an encumbrance, she deposited her ill-gotten gain {somebody else's money properly labeled and sealed} swiftly and securely into the bottom of her black patent-leather handbag. And, as if nothing out of the ordinary had occurred, she sang. She dove into the spirit, lifted her gravel-toned contralto and joined the choir in a rousing chorus of: *yoou can't beat God's givinggg...no matter how-ow you try"*

I was a little slip of a girl then, but the impression that this one act left upon my mind still fuels my opinion of churches and church folk. I still wonder how the people who tithed felt when they were accused of 'holding out' on the preacher. What did the tithers do when they learned that their money was not only uncounted, but their tithing envelope unaccounted for. I'm glad I was never that careless with my nickels and dimes!

In addition to tithes, tithing envelopes always contained a little something extra for the "building fund" or the "pastor's anniversary" or some other such worthy occasion. Those old deacons surely would let it be known which members were in financial shortfall. And, if I could see the old woman pilfering envelopes from a row back, then everybody seated on the row with her, and the ushers at each end of the row, must have seen her also. The people sitting on either side of this woman most definitely had to have noticed her bizarre behavior. Did anyone confront the old woman after church and make her give up the hefty little packages? Did the preacher know about it? If he did, did he talk to her about Christianity? And, if he didn't know, did he grill her on the Ten Commandments when he found out? Did she split the kitty with the deacons or did everyone who was *in-the-know* just let it go? She didn't look needy. That was no pauper's hat!

Impressions affix themselves to childlike minds like wallpaper. If the paste is thick and tacky, and the job well done, the walls stay papered forever, or until the paper is physically peeled off the wall. Lola Mae peeled the paper off my wall. That hypocrite! That party animal! That man stealer!

Thou shalt not steal. That's how it's written in the Bible; the book of holy words and instructions for Christians. Love thy neighbor is in there too, and nobody does that better than Lola Mae. Quiet as it's kept; she takes her role in that one far too literally. (Please don't get me started!)

The next time I see Lola Mae I hope she ain't wearing that tacky white dress with the big black flowers. If she knew how she looked in that demon thing, plastered all over with those fiendish flowers from Lucifer's garden, she would burn that hideous rag to a crisp and dump the ashes in the river, at midnight, under a full moon. The harlot!

WHOA, GLORY!

Lord! Let me pray...

THREE GLASS HEARTS

According to her neighbors, Sara Jan Mosley lived a long life. The old folks used to say she wouldn't see the high side of thirty, but she made it. She was wild in her younger years, but she made it past the predicted thirty and well into forty. At forty-seven she was older than anyone thought she would ever live to be.

It's time to bury Sara Jan now. She died Sunday morning just as the church bells started to chime. She would have been in church if she could have made it there. She would have been atoning for her sins. Atoning was ritual to her.

Sara had spent her youth drinking and carousing (that's how the old folks described it) and, in Sara's words, having fun. There was more than one man at her door in the old days, and sometimes two or three crossed paths out back.

But oddly enough, Sara fell in love. She met the one man who insisted, and told her, that she needed to "stop spinning her wheels on the oil slick of life." Herman T. she called him. His real name was Jacob, but that's another story.

Herman T. changed Sara Jan. He made her want things like a family and a little cottage with a white picket fence. She wanted grass, a garden, and a tree with a swing. And most of all, Sara wanted a baby. She wanted a part of Herman T. to hold on to for all time. Yes, Herman T. changed Sara Jan.

They wed in winter. Frost hugged the trees and a hint of snow took up residence under the cold, grey skies. It was a good time for change, this interlude before the coming tranquility of spring. They had it all. The house, the yard, peace, contentment, everything Sara had changed herself for. And, after seven years of love and laughter, Sara was pregnant. "At last," Sara squealed to Herman. She had given up every last one of her bad habits for this occasion. A baby! Their baby! They were overjoyed.

"It's a girl!" the announcement read. Six pounds seven ounces of health and beauty... The spitting image of Herman... The happy couple cried in each other's arms as they cradled their newest blessing. They named her Sheila Joy, but they called her "Blossom" for short, after Sara's flowers.

Sara doted on Blossom. Gave her everything that she herself had never had. She saddled little Blossom with boundless love. Every day was a good day and every year a perfect year until, on May 17th, at the onset of the baby's fifth year, that Tuesday of the big fire, it all ended. Sara lost them both. She lost her little Blossom, Sheila Joy; and she lost the love of her life, Herman T. Eleven years of her life came to a devastating end.

The neighbors often saw Sara at her old house, sifting through the ashes of the accident. Old Mrs. Throckmartin from next door reported that Sara wandered on and off the grounds, watering dead rose bushes with her tears. She picked mementos out of the ashes: a little metal comb that belonged to Sheila Joy's doll-baby, Emma; three brightly colored glass hearts Herman had used to win her heart when they were courting (he gave her one each time she made a great stride on the side of change); and a tightly woven Peruvian seed sack (the only keepsake to survive the tempestuous days of Sara's past). That was all that was left. Sara found them one by one in the ashes of the place she used to call home. She gathered the remains of her life and family. She put the little comb and the hearts in the seed sack and wore the sack around her neck like a diamond necklace. She was wearing it when we found her in the cemetery, her breathless body sprawled across the graves of Herman T. and Sheila Joy.

Today we buried Sara with her necklace and all of her depleted dreams.

We laid her to rest between little Blossom and her Herman T. She should rest very well there.

The neighbors say Sara looked really good.

"She looked just like herself."

That's what the neighbors say.

BEAU

She stepped out of the wheat fields with dust on her shoes and sweat on her hatband. She was a strapping woman with huge hands, big feet, and breeders' hips. Her eyes were dark and unrelenting, her jaw perfectly square. Many called her a handsome woman.

She had a flawless mahogany complexion, cocoa-brown eyes, a quick mind, and she was slow to anger. All that caught Sidney's eye and got his undivided attention. He liked everything about her, including the fact (it seemed to Sidney) that the good Lord had blessed her with the love of the entire world! She had God on her side and there wasn't a soul in the community who didn't love her. No one who didn't love being around her! She was wisdom itself! Not only did she give good advice, but she doctored all of Cotton Creek Hollow. Why, she had birthed just about all the babies in the Hollow, except for the little Sarah Nell's girl, 'cause Sarah Nell just happened to be in Button Willow when her time came and Bea'trice just couldn't get there. I think that's the only one she ever missed.

Whenever anybody took to ailing they called on Ms. Bea. "Go fetch Ms. Bea," they would instruct one of the children, and that child would scurry off to get Ms. Bea'trice and bring her wherever she was needed. Her roots and herbs were known to cure many an ache and pain. Her mysterious potions were known to save lives. Purple bushes and red vines grew in the great garden behind her house. She knew exactly what to do with her plants, how to mix and blend the cures she needed to take care of the Hollow. It was a healthy garden. Even Sidney said so.

Sidney was her match. Her soul mate. Once she set her eyes (and her mind) on Sidney, she searched his heart. When she found him true, able, and God-fearing, she let him catch her. Sidney knew it, but he didn't mind. She was his pick too. They jumped the broom in early spring and by the end of summer they had finished building a perfect cottage; just the two of them, together. Sidney was a carpenter by trade so he had say-so on the upkeep of the house. Bea'trice took charge of the grounds. It was her garden that would keep them together and thriving. Sid called her his "medicine woman." She called him "Beau," teasing him about his bow-legs.

She was thinking about Beau that morning. Bea was always thinking about Beau. She was sure of him. She wrote poems about him and folded the little scraps of paper away in a letter box wrapped in yellow ribbon. Beau was more than her husband, he was her friend. She scribbled notes in the sand for him to find. He smiled when he found them, but said nothing.

"What is it you see in Sid," her sister Della asked her that morning. "And in this old house? What is it that you think you have?"

Bea'trice looked at her sister and smiled... "I hide in the shadow of Beau's smile, Della. I am content in the shelter of his strength. It is comfortable here. It is secure and quiet where he leaves his breath for me to inhale. His movement is spiritual, deliberate. I am not startled by the stars in his eyes or by his laughter. In his smile I find release. I respond to the power in his soul. My..."

"Oh, shut-up Bea!" Della cut her off. "You are such a hopeless romantic! Please, just shut up!" She shrugged her shoulders and followed Bea'trice out the back door and into the garden. "Sid is scary," Della continued. "I worry about you, Bea."

"Scary? Why, that's just nonsense, Della. Beau is as gentle as a kitten. We have never had even a serious disagreement in all the time we've been together. Where are you getting your information? Where are these wild ideas coming from?"

"From Sweets Place, Bea. Yeah, Sid's been in there. Sid goes there often. Last Saturday evening there was a knife fight in there. Sid cut Jessie's old man across the face. He was trying to kill him, Bea."

"Oh, don't be ridiculous, Della. Beau has no reason to go to Sweets Place. Why would he be in there?"

"Gambling, Bea. Sid has taken to gambling... and other stuff."

"Sid?"

"Sid!! I can't believe you don't know what Sid is all about, Bea. You don't know Sid at all; I don't care how long you two have been together. Ask him, Bea. Ask *him* what's going on. He's not the man you knew. He's changed. Wake up, Bea! Wake up!"

Bea wanted Della to leave. She stopped short of ordering her off the property and changed the conversation to Jessie Jean's new baby. "It's due any minute now and Jessie is so huge that her feet are bad swollen," Bea reported. "That means there's gon' be trouble." She wandered to the garden and picked up her favorite wicker basket, the pale blue one that Sidney gave her last May, for her birthday. She bent over and started pulling the special plants that she would need for the birthing. As she worked the garden, Della left. When she couldn't get Bea to rally to her offensive she said goodbye and left. It was a good thing too. Bea was loosing her patience.

Bea's mind filled with questions. Not doubts, just questions.

She pushed the questions to the side and pulled her plants. She knew she had to have the right mixture of plants and herbs to stop the bleeding should Jessie Jean have problems. She collected dried astragalus, angelica and rhubarb root. She assembled sabina, arnica, and yarrow. She gathered the fruits, herbs, and other shrubs she would need to make the necessary tonics and tinctures. She harvested seeds. It was warm outside. The day was pleasant. Birds chirped away in the surrounding trees. Bea held up her hand to block the sun from her eyes and saw Sid coming up the road. She stood motionless and watched him walk. She found him graceful and regal... still. Bea tried to push back the questions but they kept crowding her and cluttering her mind. Beau. She whispered his name out loud.

She could see Beau's smile when he got close to the garden. He saw she was working and he asked about Jessie Jean. She talked to Beau about the baby but didn't go into much detail. He wouldn't understand anyway. He gave her a little peck on the top lip and went into the house. She picked up her basket of cures and followed him into the kitchen where he was pouring himself a glass of lemonade. She put her basket on the floor, poured a glass for herself and sat down. They sat face to face across the knotty-pine dinner table that Beau had built for her. Beau was really good with his hands. She didn't wait. She was not the kind of person who waited. When it came to taking care of business, Ms. Bea' took care of business.

"Della tells me you are gambling and that you are hanging out at Sweet's Place and that you cut Jessie Jean's man, Samuel Terry across the face. Is any of this true?" Beau looked straight at her. She locked onto his gaze. Bea'trice didn't know what to expect, but whatever it was, she expected the truth. "What is it, Beau? What's going on?"

Beau straightened his back and took a long, cold sip of his

lemonade. There was no way he could lie. She'd find out one way or another and he had never lied to her in all their time together. She was special. His special lady... His medicine woman... He loved her with all his heart and soul. She would understand. He didn't hesitate. He began to speak. He talked about drinking and gambling and being drunk and about sleeping with Jessie Jean and about Jessie Jean's baby and about being so sorry and about making mistakes, but never again, and about straightening himself out and about loving her like nobody's business... more than life itself.

Bea watched his mouth move. She watched him say what he had to say. She watched his mouth shape the words. She listened to the hum of the odd words and watched the ugly twisting of the corners of the mouth until something broke inside her. "This isn't Beau's mouth." As she watched, the mouth grew more and more grotesque until its hum became Satanic, so vile that it needed to be stopped. "Stop, Satan!" She had to stop the curl of Satan's lip. Something had to stop this lying; this blasphemy. She stretched her hand behind her, reaching backward until her fingers closed around the iron poker that leaned against the old coal stove. It was the first thing she found. She lifted the poker and slammed it down, and down, and down again over the twisting mouth. The mouth finally went still. Silent. And then there was nothing. The humming stopped. Bea wrapped both her arms around her body and rocked herself. She rocked back and forth. There was blood in her lemonade. She wondered how it got there. She rocked herself gently and hummed her mother's favorite hymn: *Rock of ages cleft for me ... Let me hide myself in thee ...*

**

Bea'trice Wilson had been in Tennessee State Hospital eight years when she died. Eight years and she never knew she was

51

there. She didn't know where she was or who she was. Della came to see her sister every first Sunday. Bea didn't know Della. She didn't know anyone. She wandered around the hospital grounds with a blue wicker basket. She pulled up the plants if nobody stopped her. The nurses had a hard time when they took her outside. She loved the grounds, but she insisted on pulling the plants.

"These plants are for Jessie Jean", she told the nurses.

"Jessie Jean will need these plants."

"These plants are for Jessie Jean."

YESTERDAY

Stars twinkle in the distance and a bell-like jingle flirts with songs on the breeze. I look toward the hills behind the barn and see you working the fields like tomorrow is not coming and nightfall is already upon us.

We never have time to sing the songs we once wrote - you and me. A bowl of love and cherries, that's how it once was. That's how it used to be.

The songs are still here, in the box behind the bed stand, next to the empty crib. Our songs. Our life together bound in rose colored ribbon and faded yellow paper. Songs from back in the day. Songs from when your smile was everything that *happy* meant.

"Dinner," I call out to you. "DINNER!"

You never hear me calling anymore.

I wish you didn't work so hard.

I wish you didn't work as if there is only yesterday.

FIRST MEETING

He came across the hill and was walking in the shadow of the moon when I saw him; tall, slender, and moving gracefully toward the center of town.

He ain't from around here! I know everybody here, there's so few of us.

I watch him from my silent spot in the darkness, from the lawn chair I pulled to the side of Grandma Moochie's porch onto the path by the rose trellises. It's a good spot to sit and think. No one in the house can see me and I don't have to walk out into the gardens or the fields and take chances with snakes. Most folks swear snakes sleep at night, but I'm not so sure of that.

Anyway, the closer he gets the more the moonlight frames his face. He can't see me but I can see him. His face is the color of copper pennies. Brand new copper pennies. And his skin is smooth like fresh ironing. He has a look that is very easy on the eye.

I watch him get closer and closer. His clothes fit him well. The cuffs of his trousers tip his shoestrings and clip the back of the shoe just above the heel. The shoes shine even in the moonlight. He stands straight, and his head reaches into the moon. He must be at least 6'8". I am in love!

The rhythm in his stride pulls my shoulders from the back of the chair. I prepare to lift myself out of the darkness. A few more strides and he'll be in front of the house, right outside the gate.

My connection to the lawn chair is broken. In less time than it takes to make the decision to get up, I make my way to the gate. I am floating there when he arrives. I hear myself speak:

"New around here aren't you. I'm not. And I'm the best friend you'll ever have here. I can show you around. And make sure you don't get into trouble. Not married are you. You're not wearing a ring. Wanna get married. I'll marry you. Try me. You'll see. You won't be disappointed. I love you..."

And that is where we will end this.

Jeannette DesBoine

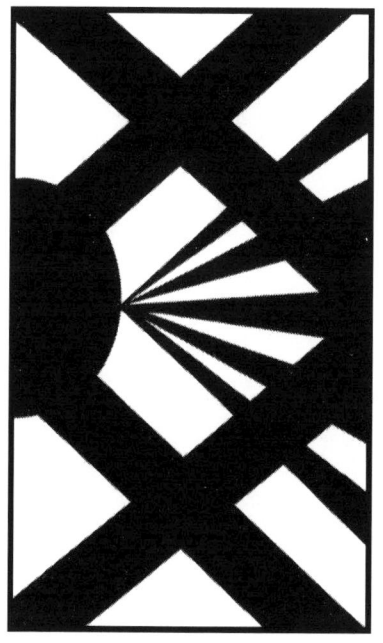

THREE

THE TRI-POD STORY

"It's a pleasure talking to you Mrs. Johnson. Hope to see you in church Sunday morning."

She walked away mumbling to herself (something about a camera on a tri-pod, I think) but she managed to throw up her hand to issue a curt goodbye wave as she stumbled across the sizzling parking lot.

That was the last time I saw her. It was Thursday afternoon. We stood in line at Earle's (the best barbecue place for miles around) and talked for quite a while. At least *she* talked, and I tried to concentrate on what she was saying. The July holiday line was long. It's cool inside Earle's. He has the best air conditioner in town. Refrigerated air! You can bet he wracks up the bucks in the summer months. Lots of folks come in just to get out of the heat. They sit and visit and eat in the cool. It beats cooking.

I stacked our dinner in the back of the Trooper and drove to the park to pick up the kids from the school picnic. The baseball game was ending just as I got there. My little ones came running across the field all excited and eagerly telling me how they won the game, and how many hits they got, and who messed up and who didn't. Dust flew off their little uniforms and cleats as they bounced into the back seat.

"Kiss, kiss!" I half shouted at them over the noise of their excitement. "Buckle up!" I was saying as they automatically fastened their seat belts.

"No school tomorrow! No school tomorrow!" they chanted as we pulled away from the curb and headed home.

"Turn up the air, Mom."

"You missed a good game, Mommy."

"Yeah, Mom. Real good."

"The best! We tied for first place!"

Mrs. Johnson wasn't in church that Sunday morning. At least she wasn't at Emmanuel Baptist. Everybody asked about her and promised to call her after church just to check on her. She sure missed a good service. Pastor Daniels lit a fire under those pews that day. The junior choir sang all new songs and performed a *rap* for the Lord, which they wrote in their Bible study class. They had been working on that rap for three months, and when Sis. Beverly, their director, turned them loose with her blessings, they truly performed. The church-house was full of amen's and hallelujahs.

It was Tuesday when I got the news that Mrs. Johnson had died. Almost a week to the day that I had seen her at the barbecue place where she was telling me about her grandson Joshua, who was coming home.

She seemed a little anxious as she told me about Josh, who was eighteen now and had been away since he was fourteen. He had gotten into serious trouble, she said, and ended up spending four years in jail. She talked about his "wrong friends;" how he wouldn't listen; his gang-banging and fast living; about drugs, drug dealing, and the death of one of his so-called friends in a drive-by. Her speech was so labored that it was hard to understand her. She breathed like she'd been running, and she was perspiring even while standing under the air. I figured she was distracted and nervous about her grandson's return.

I didn't know Mrs. Johnson all that well. She started coming to our church about four years ago. She didn't make it every Sunday, but she was a regular member. She joined church on June 23 at Tuesday night prayer meeting. It was my best friend's birthday, that's how I remember. Mrs. Johnson told the meeting that she "came to learn how to pray." She was in prayer meeting every Tuesday night since. Never missed one Tuesday. I saw her there occasionally (I didn't go every Tuesday like she did) and I saw her at Sunday morning services whenever she chose to come.

I guess I should have seen that Mrs. Johnson was not feeling well that day at Earle's, but it just never entered my mind. She never complained about anything, and as far as anyone knew, she was in good health. Nevertheless, I should have gotten a clue from her heavy perspiration, the slurred speech, and the way she sort of staggered across the parking lot. Well, she's gone now, God rest her soul!

Joshua James Gregory spoke at his grandmother's funeral. He spoke proudly and distinctly. That's when I got the whole story:

> *My grandmother, Mrs. Alberta Johnson, was sick when I left home - an inoperable heart condition. Grandma was all I had. When I went to jail, she promised she would be here for me when I got back, no matter what. That was a big promise coming from a woman who knew she was dying, but grandma was always bigger than life itself. At least to me.*
>
> *Alberta Johnson did all she could do to keep me out of trouble. She did not succeed because I did not listen. But Grandma was not a woman who gave up easily. When I left, she said she would pray for me. I looked into her eyes, past the tears, and thought: 'Pray? When did you start*

praying?' *I didn't say that out loud, but, I never knew grandma to pray! She was not a church-going woman, not at the time, and she had never been a church-going woman as far as I knew.*

She must have known what I was thinking. She looked deep into my defiant eyes, took both my hands in hers, and told me very calmly: "I am going to pray for you. I am going to go to church and learn to pray. I've tried everything else. Let's try God."

Grandma didn't get around well so she didn't visit me in jail. But she wrote me, and I kept all her letters. A letter a month for four years. Forty eight letters. I kept them in a shoe box. They all say the same thing. "Try God." At first I didn't think much of the letters. I just threw them in the shoe box. I resented the fact that the letters never said anything but 'Try God.' My name wasn't even on them. No 'Dear Josh'. No 'Love, Grandma'. Just TRY GOD in big block letters.

Somewhere in the second year I began to look forward to what I began to call "the letter". For some reason I sensed a feeling of calm moving into my life. One day I showed up in vespers. There was a group of evangelists who came every week to minister to those who chose to participate. To make a long story short, I began to study religion. I don't know when God chose me, but I studied for the ministry through a program offered at the facility. I'm eighteen. I got my G.E.D., found God, and received a certifi-

cate of divinity all in jail. Grandma did all that for me because she never gave up on me. When they took me away that day, Grandma told me to try God. She did, and I did too.

Grandma never mentioned her illness. She never let me know how things were going on the outside. She just sent "the letter" that changed my life. I remember her saying that she would be waiting for me when I got back. I thought maybe she would die first, but as long as the letters came I held on with faith to the promise that she had made to me.

I was never so glad to see anybody as I was to see Grandma Johnson when I got home. She had my favorite meal. She had been to Earle's and loaded us up with the best barbecue in town. She ate very little, and while I ate I told her who I was. We talked all through supper and when we had finished I presented Grandma with a present I had created for just this occasion. On my way home I had all forty-eight of her letters framed as a thank you gift for her. She cried when she opened the box. She had me hang all the letters on her dining room wall. She watched me as I worked. "This is where I prayed for you," she told me. "Right here at this table. In this very chair. Every day and every night. Hang the frames so they face this chair. This will be your seat from now on." She talked business to me, about the house and my future. She gave me a stack of papers and said that everything I needed was in that stack of papers and the details were downtown at the office of Attorney Rivers.

Peace entered her face, and through tears and smiles and thank you(s) to God, she let me know that she was happy with who I had become. She told me she would rest then, and she went to her room to lie down. She asked me to make a big glass of lemon julep and bring it to her. I got lemons off her tree in the back yard and made a pitcher of the syrupy sweet lemonade she called julep, just the way she taught me when I was little. I brought her favorite serving tray, the pitcher, and two frosted glasses to her bedside. I propped her up on her pillows and poured us both a big, icy glass full. She sipped the julep and said it was very good. She told me that she loved me and was proud of me. She said she knew that everything would be fine with me from now on and that she felt that she could leave me and go on to her 'higher journey,' as she called it. Grandma was going to leave me then. I knew this. She had stayed with me through thick and thin. She held on just for me. She brought me from the depths of despair and set me on solid ground. We talked quietly into the evening. She laughed as I reminded her of some of the good things I remembered from the old days. Some of the better times we had shared. We laughed together. I held her hand. I rocked her in my arms when she seemed weak and short of breath. I traveled with her as far as I could go as she began her journey.

Late that evening she touched my cheek, kissed me, told me what a wonderful man God had made me, and she said goodbye. There was an echo around her room. The voice was hers, and it repeated three times: Try God. Try God. Try God. Then she was gone. I can still see her eyes dimming.

Grandma will always be with me no matter what. I thank God for my Grandmother and for her letters encouraging me to try God.

I love you Grandma. Rest in Peace. Go with God and rest in peace.

**

I thought about what Josh had said. For days after the funeral I thought about his life and Mrs. Johnson's life. It's funny how little we actually know another person, even though they're part of our community. Then it hit me! That's what Mrs. Johnson was saying that day when she waved goodbye to me at Earle's. It wasn't about a camera or a tripod or any such nonsense as I had thought. What she was saying was: "Try God." Lord, what an amazing woman!

"Mom, we're going to be late for the game!" The shouts of my two little ballplayers broke my reverie. "Come on," they were shouting, "you don't want to miss this game; it's the playoffs."

I brought myself back into the present and grabbed my car keys. "Okay, girls, come on, I'm ready!" "Where is your brother?" "Andrew went to church with his new friend, Josh," they informed me.

Josh is Youth Minister at Emmanuel, and the church has given him a scholarship to continue his education at the school of theology. What an outstanding young man.

Sister Johnson sure raised him right.

MEMORY IS A MUSCLE

Memory is a muscle. Sometimes flabby and weak. Sometimes strong and powerful. Always in a state of flux. Changing. From passive to aggressive. From clear to vague.

Memory is a friend sometimes and an enemy at other times. Memory is inconsistent. Cannot be controlled. Will not be manipulated.

Sometimes memory hides in dark corners. Sometimes it dances in the brightest light. Sometimes it whispers on a gentle breeze or blows gale winds through cypress trees.

Memory may ripple down a bouncing stream or foam and lather in a raging sea. It may be flexible. It may be stiff. Inspiration or aggravation. It sometimes wrestles with recognition and often plays games with its own definition. It's on again off again. It comes and goes. It's up. It's down. It's in and out. But memory is always female.

Memory leaves dim lights in wastelands. We follow the winding light down faded paths leading to bolted doors. Sometimes memory is coquettish! A tease! A common trollop! Vicious in her abstinence.

Memory has multiple personalities. Sometimes she's an ally, sometimes an adversary.

Memory is bipolar. And dangerous if allowed to run rampant without her medications.

Memory walks upright. She runs, jumps, and crawls. She's the composer and the bridge in her own compositions.

Memory writes her own epitaphs, then erases what she has written and draws fuzzy pictures which never seem to come together, or to end.

Memory inhabits sizable shelters, or may be contained in ethereal closets, but if you really listen you can hear her giggling, her laughter like wind-chimes embracing the breeze.

Memory lives a long time. I think she may be immortal. When she reaches back in time we call her long-term. When she confines herself to current events we label her short-term. Memory turns herself on and off at will, like a light switch or a timer. Memory has that power!

Sometimes I wonder if memory is deliberately selective or if she is controlled by some outside source, some power even higher than she herself, some entity far superior to her limitations, to her aspirations. And I question her intentions. Is she with me or against me? Does she love or hate me? Is she real or unreal?

Questions race through my soul. When doubt enters my mind I wrap my head around concept. Is she friend? Is she foe? Cohort or competitor? Hypocrite or authentic? Serious or a joke?

Is she young? Is she old? Is she then? Is she now? Is she good? Is she evil? Is she fact? Is she fiction? Is she REAL?

I often question her validity, but in the final analysis I realize that no matter what memory is or isn't, she is mine. She belongs to me!

And that simple fact soothes me.

PRIME TIME

She was in her prime. She knew it, but Harold refused to agree. There were many unspoken words between them until one day she had just had it. Enough was enough. Who did he think he was anyway? He was just *Harold*. It wasn't like he was her father or anything, or could tell her who *she* was and what *she* was all about. Even dear-old-dad couldn't have done that; God rest his ornery soul.

Today was the day. She felt like a million dollars. Everything was going great. She was in full flow. Her world was that oyster that everybody talks about and she needed no permission-slip to enter, explore, and enjoy her own oyster.

Harold was in his normal position, propped up in front of the television, feet on the coffee table, cigarette smoke curling around his flat head, a Budweiser at arm's length on the floor beside the recliner. The score was 7 to 6. The Raiders were at the goal line. The kicker positioned himself. Harold perched on the edge of his seat. This would tie it up! The stadium was going wild. Harold dangled on the edge of hysteria, first holding his breath, then hyperventilating.

Lynette felt her moment. Now was the time. She floated across the room and abruptly hit the off switch. When the TV went black, Harold went crazy.

"HEY!!"

"WHAT THE HELL ARE YOU DOING?"

His skin was so red it actually glowed and radiated heat around the living room. Harold choked, sputtered and coughed up beer suds. "TURN THAT BACK ON! TURN IT ON! HURRY! I'M MISSING THE PLAY!"

Lynette smiled and stood in front of the set with her arms folded across her chest. Harold was half-way off the recliner when Lynette unfolded her arms and spread them open, gesturing Harold to come into those wide open arms. Into that embrace. The unusual posture startled Harold. He didn't know whether to move toward her or away from her. The look in her eye read: challenge. Harold lowered himself back onto the edge of the recliner. He looked at Lynette for a sensible moment and said: "Could you turn the TV back on?" He asked her gently; calmly; nicely.

"Sure thing, Harold," Lynette answered, "whatever you want." She switched on the television and flipped the dial to the soap opera channel, tuning in just in time to hear the announcer smoothly croon: "... and these are the Days of Our Lives."

Still smiling sweetly, Lynette walked over to the recliner, nudged, wiggled, and wedged her square hips in next to Harold. She lifted his beer arm, snuggled up under him, gave him a little peck on the cheek and whispered in his ear: "Who's your baby, baby?"

Harold he knew he couldn't win. He gave up all resistance. He slouched down in the chair, locked his livid eyes onto the TV screen, gritted his teeth and collapsed into the current trauma of "Days of Our Lives."

Lynette handed him his inhaler.

UNFINISHED BUSINESS

She was the kind of person who prayed out loud. There was no shame in her game. She claimed to have a personal relationship with her God, but I had my doubts. "My God in covenant with me," she scolded as she bent down to put more bleach in the bathtub. She could never get that thing clean enough to suit her standards. It didn't shine quite right. "Hard water is the devils workshop," she said to nobody in particular, and she scrubbed and scrubbed until her knuckles were raw. She had ditch-digger hands.

We heard someone calling. She got up and went to the door. I tried to recognize the figure out front. I strained my eyes and finally distinguished Naomi's daughter, Jessica, leaning on the gate. "Give me strength, Master..." Naomi whispered under her breath as she rolled her narrow eyes toward heaven. The plea on her lips matched the stiffness in her spine. I got a chill in my own heart, not that it wasn't good to see Jessica again after all these years but, well, I'm just saying.

Awful memories flooded my air. Addiction, solicitation, restraining orders, prison, you name it! I gave memory a brief minute then dismissed it. After all, she wasn't my child. I could only imagine what Naomi was feeling. The two of them had survived some extremely hard times.

Jessica looked the same. Well, almost the same. Well, not really. She looked hard. With a little more weight on her long frame and a hump in the bridge of her once perfectly shaped nose. A bad break. I held that picture in my mind for a moment, trying to imagine how Jessica would manage to get her nose crushed like that.

Naomi inventoried her estranged daughter carefully. We both noticed that her shoulders were just a tad more rounded where they once were rigidly square. Jessica looked old. Way older than her thirty years. "Life has taken its toll!" Naomi told God. "Life-style has done the rest." I knew she wasn't talking to me. She forgot I was even there.

The clothes Jessica had on did not appear to be hers. They *almost* fit, but the buttons on the faded cotton blouse were strained across bulging breast tissue. The polyester suit had seen better days but it now told its history in frays, pill-balls, and runs. And she wore someone else's shoes. That was obvious in the open space behind the heel. Way too long.

So, she's back. Home again? For what? Why?

"Father I stretch my hand to thee..." Naomi prayed earnestly as she waited for her child to drag herself across the lawn to the shade of the porch where she waited, unsure, cautious, paralyzed except for the twitch in her left eye. She watched Jessica limp and labor across the yard. *"Lord, she is trampling my ivy."* Naomi stiffened. I could feel her blood pressure rise.

"Good morning, Mama," the hoarse voice croaked across several small patches of milkweed. "Can I come in, Mama? I need to sit down. It's mighty hot out here, mama. Can I come in and sit down?"

Jessica inched closer and closer. Movement was obviously not easy for her. When she finally reached the landing she looked up at Naomi with a tear in her eye. She lifted her right hand and stretched it toward her mother. She put one foot on the stairs and clenched the railing in her left hand.

"Lord, give me strength!" Naomi mumbled under her breath as Jessica transferred her weight onto the ball of her left foot. She clenched her jaw. I could hear her teeth grinding.

Jessica's heart echoed the same sentiments as her mother's. "Give me strength, Lord," she muttered as she began pulling herself slowly up her mother's stairs – not knowing if she would be welcome or not...

I held my breath and called on the grace of God.

Lord, help us! I prayed.

Lord, help us.

FEATHERS

She hadn't realized that the feather droppings were from her wings. Nor did she know that she *had* wings, everything was new to her. This was a new world, a new reality, a new morality.

Feathers. Where did they come from? Where were the innocent beginnings that told her that she, unlike the rest of the girls in the world, was special? She never knew what made her special other than the many times she heard her mother call her an angel. She was as pure as silent snow, she heard said of her, and when she heard this she believed it. She heard it so much that she began to see herself as the angel her mother described.

She drifted inside herself and built a shelter clouded over by occasional self-doubt. But she shoved the clouds away as often as they gathered. Finally, she felt the weight of expectation tug at her back. It tightened around her shoulder blades and knotted up. From there a growth started. When it broke the skin, she was afraid to tell anyone. She was afraid there was something wrong. Afraid she had *done* something wrong. The growth continued. It started slowly but progressed with alarming speed. Wings. She discovered wings.

The mirror verified it. Wings! Oh, how will I keep them hidden, she worried. She wore the most unusual clothes. But nobody knew.

Then the feathers began to drop. She guessed it was a seasonal thing. Like molting. And the clothes got bigger. And the wings got bigger. And heavier. And she hid herself away from prying eyes until that final day when her mother found her angel squatting over a tiny angel of her own. The feather droppings gave the whole thing away.

"Truth" was the feather dropped from her wings.

SIDRAH'

She has her moments. Times when laughter overcomes her. When the sweet round eyes of children tickle her pink and the rough burlap sacks she clips, cleans, and fashions into kitchen curtains diffuses the harsh light of day until the future is easy to see.

She knows. She's blessed with sacred knowledge, and that knowledge (which was once a burden) no longer frightens her. Knowing is powerful.

She welcomes her power and relies on her visions. The power is friendly. It guides, strengthens, and provides. The power pulverizes anger and tears, and chisels laugh lines as deep as canals into her remarkable face. Her eyes sparkle with a wisdom that only joy can penetrate. She is known as Help, and her name is Sidrah'.

Yes, Help is her title as well as her mission in life. "One cannot be sad when concern is placed outside the self." That's what she teaches and I believe her. I have watched her work. I have received and welcomed her. She moves with the grace of cooling waters.

Listen! Can't you hear the water fall?

Sidrah' is her given name, but never call her Sid in front of strangers. "The burden of familiarity belongs to me," she will admonish. And she is firm in this even though she smiles that infectious smile as she speaks.

I respect her wishes and adhere to her commands. She is Help. The only help I know. She is teaching me to smile. Soon, she says, I will know when to laugh right out loud.

I can hardly wait!

Thank you, Sidrah'.

Oh, thank you so very much.

THE GODDESS

She once spread trees with her wide hips and squatted in the fields to give birth to the world.

Today her hair hangs like leaves, limply cascaded over her burdened shoulders.

She watches the horizon, waiting and listening for the proper time to suckle her universe.

While she waits she contemplates, her head bowed slightly as if in guilt, or shame.

She peers from behind slit eyelids. There is a darkness, a dullness there, in her spirit. It gives way to motive. She shuts her eyes and sighs.

The first voice makes her aware of her surroundings. She listens to the whispers.

"She is loosing her touch. Becoming predictable!"

"She is too easily read by the slightest of the slight. The ones she so detests."

"She's lost her edge. She's gone."

"She's taken to underachieving. That's her watchword. She's doing more than is called for, but not at all well. She's lost ground. She might as well say goodbye."

Her ankles, swollen from crouching in weeds, look ready to pop with the slightest touch. Her knees, blue with pain, are only a bit less swollen than the rest of her. Confusion shakes her. Right? Wrong? What? Why? She clasps her hands and assumes the position.

"She's down in the ankles and weak in the knees."

"Her gun-sights are not as accurate as they once were."

"Her dagger is dull compared to the days when she was quick as silver and sharp as a tack."

"She's gone I tell you! She's a modern mess!"

"Goodbye you old witch!"

"Aim for her feet," they cackle. *"Kick her in the ankles!"*

"Go for the knees!"

"Kill! KILL! KILL!"

They make their move and her posture shifts. The shift is casual, but when *she* moves, all other movement ceases. Aside from a universal gasp, silence becomes the new watchword.

And then her voice occurs. It is silky and sincere: "EVERY SHUT EYE AIN'T SLEEP!" it cautions, "AND EVERY GOODBYE AIN'T GONE!"

Moral:

Foolishness induces overconfidence; egomania breeds errors; and mistakes are not only unforgiving, but often fatal.

CROSSFIRE

I'm not positive how it happened last Sunday morning, but I was there when that thick, green cloud lumbered low in the skies. With it, a strange warm breeze and an intoxicating odor came from the refinery at the west end of town. The smelly breeze caught our stale southern air in crossfire. There was no escaping it. People have to breathe, and as we inhaled, the whole town went wild. Strange gasses filled the streets and seeped under window sills. Soon, a toxic confusion overtook our town; the people and the animals. That acidic confusion also settled over Georgia Street's First Baptist Church, causing the choir to sing its songs of contentment in, of all things, the key of *G*! The choir never sings in *G*! There are no *G* voices!

First Baptist is a conservative church. Sophisticated. Undemonstrative. "Boogie" some say; but on this day the congregation stood (one by one) and joined hands. (This was a first.)

"Praise be! Praises unto Him! Praise His name!" The deacons jumped for joy. They hooped and hollered. Hallelujah's oozed from the tight-lipped ushers. "Hallelujah! Glory be! Glory to His name!" The sound of song rose until it shook the stained glass windows. *WE ARE SOLDIERS ... IN THE ARMY ...* Reverend Whitney took the lectern. He lifted his huge right hand and waved it to and fro like a signal lamp while his congregation mimicked the rhythm, moving back and forth in response to his rhythm of guidance. (Another first!)

Whitney began his sermon. "Today we shall speak of tithing", he advised. *"SHALL A MAN ROB GOD?"* Whitney blasted the thunder-filled query off the rafters. It ricocheted the lightening of accusation. The flock hissed its reaction to the subject matter. I smiled and kept silent, but I liken that hissing to the hiss of the serpent of the Garden of Eden! Organ music accentuated Whitney's preacher-points with sharp, shrill crescendos that highlighted important words like *thief, saints*, and *sinners*. The good reverend detonated his theme, mesmerized his audience, and shackled his people to the Word of God. When Whitney was all lathered up and the flock fully captured, the music stopped. The organist left her station and proudly took her assigned front row seat. (That organist knows her job really well. That's why she makes the big bucks.)

"I talked to God last night," Reverend Whitney reported, "and God told me to tell you..." And, believe it or not, the organ chimed loudly at that very moment. All by itself. Not a soul was sitting there. The organist had already assumed her first-pew seating. The congregation looked at the organist then we looked at each other. Every eye in the church was stretched wide with awe and wonder. Every church member, including me, whispered urgent amen's in salute to the power of God.

It's a sign! It's a sign! That's what we felt and communicated one to another. Reverend Whitney evidently saw the chime of the organ as a sign also. He sucked in his breath and leaped wholeheartedly into his theme. "Shall a man rob God?" he repeated in no uncertain terms.

"Preach Rev!" "Say it, now!" "Tell the truth!" The crowd was drawn into the mood. But moments into the message the excitement died, and like bees in the monotone of a Gregorian chant, repetitive snoring emitted from Deacon's Row. It was hypnotic. Infectious! A paralyzing white noise. An eclectic buzz. Half the congregation was asleep. The rest, including me, had taken on some sort of comatose state. I felt conscious. I could see what was happening but I couldn't respond.

Elder Green led the snoring. Deacon Andrews led the refrain. The church body joined in. (zzz) Asleep! Out cold! Unconscious! We were all out of it in some way. Either asleep or catatonic!

Reverend Whitney was confused. He tried to get louder but the congregation got louder still. He dropped to a more quiet tone and the congregation purred in unison. He tried a bit of pulpit psychology. *"YA'LL DON'T HEAR ME!"* he shrieked. The crowd sputtered, cleared their throats, sucked in new air and settled into more synchronized snoring. *"What's happening, Lord?"* I heard the question, but no answer. The sermon ended. The snoring drowned the reverend out. *"My eyes are burning and I feel dizzy. What's happening here?"* Rev. Whitney was talking out loud. I heard him but I couldn't respond.

Well, to finish the story, Whitney credits his dizziness to the Spirit. He says he didn't know if he was speaking out loud or thinking to himself at the time. He was surveying the congregation for resolution and signs of life when, from the middle pews, he spied a pair of conscious eyes. "Big, brown, pie plate eyes!" he says. Huge, innocent eyes! Intent, wise eyes!" Well, the electricity of those eyes obviously caught and held Whitney's attention. He locked onto that gaze and, for some reason, he says, there was a lull in the congregational hum. The reverend watched a tiny little girl begin to inch forward on the bench. She wriggled her way to the edge of her seat, stretched her legs and pointed her toes until her feet were close enough to the floor to hop down. The big, brown eyes widened even more as she stood up and stretched her neck so she could see over the back of the pew in front of her. She stared sympathetically at Whitney and raised her right hand. A delicate little index finger extended purposefully towards heaven and a determined little voice issued the Reverend a firm, but adorable: *"Amen!"*

RIOT AT REASON'S DOOR
(a bedtime story with a moral)

> *this is a horror story*
> *but read it if you dare*
> *it may get a little gory*
> *but I tell it because I care*

well now, Laughter and Joy were husband and wife
    the fruit of the union of Peace and Delight
their children were many, their family strong
    they all will be mentioned as you follow along

you see, Gloom and Doom were a couple
    as deemed by common-law
with so many illegitimate off-spring
    that I cannot name them all

there was Chaos, Confusion,
    there was Grief and Despair,
there was Death and Destruction,
    all spawned by this pair

> *this is not a pretty story*
> *it's a discourse of disdain*
> *it's a tale of pain and sorrow*
> *let me warn you once again*

well, Gloom and Doom sneaked into the room
    and switched off the light on Happy and Bright
but Gloom and Doom unlike thieves in the night
    never supposed such a horrible fight

the melee was on!
        a battle ensued!
as Laughter and Joy
        waged war

"Gloom and Doom get out of our space
        you're not welcome in this place
we won't let you stay, not even one day
        get out! be on your way!"

Joy tossed Gloom across the room
        where he landed in a heap
Hope joined the fray, punching and kicking
        until Gloom, without doubt, was taking a licking

with the roar of a lion in search of fresh food,
        Glee drop-kicked Doom, inflicting deep wounds
with fire in her eye, Mirth sauntered by,
        crashing great blows to Doom's head
a quick glimpse at Doom from the back of the room
        and one would have sworn she was dead

before Doom knew it little Happy was in it...
        snarling and scratching and biting
Happy choked Doom until she was blue
        and then she grabbed one of the others

Gloom and Doom had invaded their space
        and they were not going to have it
Laughter and Mirth (for all they were worth)
        fought to protect their palace

Peace and Joy and Merriment
        were having none of this devilment!
Doom and Gloom had invaded their space
        and, oh, were they sorry they had come to this place

they were beaten and clubbed
        outnumbered and snubbed
just like Chaos, and Grief, and Confusion

Smiley whipped out a razor sharp blade
        and slit the throat of Sorrow
"you'll get the same thing if ya'll come back again
        so forget about tomorrow"

Levity latched onto Misery
        and gave her neck a snap
Harmony, in the meanwhile
        had broken Apathy's back

with a powerful grip, Joy took a whip
        to Gloom and all his descendents...
bodies and parts were so scattered and tossed
        it took weeks to bury the remnants

I'll spare you the gore and tell you no more
of the brawl I remember yet
but had you been there to witness,
you too, would never forget

this story has a moral
and this is what is found
when you find Joy and Laughter
do not put them down

for they will fight with all their might
and never give up the ghost
their pride is strong, their commitment long
and never do they boast

this is a tale of disaster
when Death threatened Joy and Laughter
when all of their young (even Hope's unborn)
fought to defend their castle

Gloom and Doom met their master
while Laughter and Joy lived happily after
Mirth and her many, many kin
beat back Disaster again and again

it's a fact that Misery craves company
while Joy has her way with Peace
as Contentment plots your life's journey
just be careful the company you keep

Jeannette DesBoine

FOUR

RAILS

I walk the railroad tracks listening for the whistle of a train; instinctively sniffing the air for change; my feet anticipating the rumbling of the rails. The ground is solid and warm under the thin soles of my shoes. I have walked long and far on this path; through big cities, small towns, and pit-stops in the path of progress. Unlimited travel is a perpetual fling!

I stop at a library to cool my heels, to quench my thirsts, to void and such. Young children swing on railings, run the edifice side to side, front to back, and incessantly bounce rubber balls while neither parent nor librarian calls ceasefire. I remember a time when library meant quiet. I guess that was long ago and far away in a different set of values.

At a nearby playground, a two-year-old plays unattended while her father, his back to the child, holds lengthy flirtations with three new moms. His child takes a hard fall and a stranger picks her up just as she exhales the shrill screams. In far too many split seconds the dad remembers his child, recognizes her cry, realizes her distress, and comes to her aide. Sometimes daddies are nothing more than unobserving, undeserving sperm donors.

Then there are teachers and preachers who contradict formulae in favor of personal compromise. Stand in any such courtyard and observe. They look askance at reason and implement self-directed change as if eons of rules are inconsequential. They contrive red badges of wisdom from renal paradigm.

But, all in all, paradise is still a wheat field void of vermin baked into the bread of life. Still a sandwich with no unidentified crunch and no indeterminable crumbs!

All in all, a never ending journey!

Walk the railroad tracks.

Listen for the whistle of a train.

OLD SOLDIERS

Arthur A. Benton
Sergeant Major
U. S. Army (Ret)

Arthur Benton, a broken and struggling old man with scraggily gray eyebrows and burnt, withered skin had a penchant for telling war stories about foxholes and flags to all who would listen.

Every morning, without fail, Sgt. Major Benton dug a new hash-mark in a dingy southern wall in the dank room he now called home. He did this with a World War I drawing knife that he somehow managed to keep hidden from hospital authorities. How Benton got this souvenir into the facility was a secret locked inside a bruised mind.

Benton's hash-marks count and calculate time. A corroded metal picture frame, the size of a deck of playing cards, accentuates the chips in the concrete wall. The picture frame contains an old, yellow, faded photograph of a flamboyant and proud young Arthur Benton in uniform, marching off to war. His long slender arm waves a hearty goodbye to someone long forgotten. There are no other pictures in the room and all of Arthur's other memories seem to be locked deeply inside his own understanding.

The war had labeled Sgt. Major Benton cowardly and psychotic. There were those to whom the "pitiful old codger" appeared angry, fearful, lonely and demented. Obsessive! A mad-man! And then there were those to whom his staggering speeches about war crimes and internal atrocities earned him even more dubious disdain.   Descriptions of Author Benton ranged from manic, to mean and obnoxious, to the most familiar: "one crazy bastard."

Benton was not a gentle man. He had never been a gentle man, and the cocky young soldier learned a lot of bad habits in service to his country. He returned excited, excitable, and telling many a strange story of kidnap, murder, and buried evidence.

These days, there aren't too many of his comrades left alive to corroborate, let alone listen to, Arthur Benton's stories. And even less who care. That is, until the kid started coming around.

This is the youngsters' first real job. And although it isn't for the biggest newspaper in town, he is, officially, a reporter, and proud of it.

He takes out his notebook, pulls the pencil from behind his ear, switches on the new tape recording device and takes a seat next to an extremely agitated Arthur Alexander Benton, Sergeant Major, United States Army (Retired).

"It ain't over I tell you boy!" Benton screams at the top of his lungs. "That's what they want you to think.   But you believe me boy; listen to what I'm telling you!   This war ain't nowhere near over!   Not on your goddamn life..."

...

BEST BUDDIES

We are going in no matter what! The storm is treacherous, but the ships lumber steadily toward the beach as the thunderous white-light of artillery fire and bursting bombs stir blood in the sea and rattle our bones and teeth. It is D-Day, June 6, 1944, 6:30 p.m., Omaha Beach, Normandy, WWII. The mortar fire splits my eardrums. Our infantry lands and our troops drop into the water and wallow through bodies and gore to a blistered, shell-shocked shore. Strong winds have blown us east of our intended landing positions, leaving us wading through a perilous airborne assault. D-Day! In my mind I translate that to Death-Day, but I keep going through the lightening-streaked skies and thick, black smoke that blisters my lungs with the fury of fire.

We are ground troops. Infantry. Mud soldiers. A fighting brigade with too many bodies already scattered helter-skelter from ship to shore. Stepping over death becomes ordinary. We are under fire so heavy that the thought of making it to the actual battlefield seems impossible. We are loaded down. In full battle gear. Rifles that we can't point and shoot on the crawl. Grenades that dangle from our hips like decoys. And useless helmets that cannot, and do not, stop mortar rounds. We can't see the enemy from here, nor do we know the distance of their encampment or the range of their weapons, which are laying waste to our forces. Carlos and I ditch the ship and drop into the water together. Body parts drift around us and keep us together as they bobble and float on the tide. Carlos tries to keep me calm as destruction takes my mind. When we reach the beach we stumble in the muck and mire, pull ourselves upright, stand as tall as we dare and haul for cover, our boots and uniforms dripping blood.

I am behind Carlos. I am always behind Carlos. In high school Carlos ran the dash in 9.4. A natural leader.

We are a long way from Texas; a long way from Abilene High School; and a long way from the 3rd grade when C.J. (Carlos Jimenez) pulled Charlie Sosa off me for the third time. This time Carlos broke Charlie's nose. That was the last beating I had to take from Charlie. He was humiliated by the laughter of all the kids in Cebada Projects.

Charlie was a big dude, and he was mean, and he always wanted a piece of me. But after that incident, when C.J. broke his nose, C.J. and I became running-buddies. If you saw one of us you saw the other. C.J. was always around to protect me. I followed him everywhere. I even followed him to the recruiting office where we enlisted together and became members of the same outfit. Now bombs burst the air over our heads and I know this is it! This is the end! I am afraid. Petrified! I want to vomit. I crouch down behind Carlos and follow him up the beach and onto the countryside. I follow until Carlos falls. I roll him into a hole and I drop down beside him. We lay like that, side by side, pinned down by the thunder and lightening of war for I don't know how long, maybe minutes, maybe hours, forever. When I come to my senses I take off my belt and cinch it around what is left of C.J.'s right leg. I hunker down and train my rifle on danger. I cannot and will not leave him.

The sun rises and sets so many times I lose count. It's dark when I hear movement and brace my weapon to fight to the death. I grit my teeth, lock them together and stare into the blackness. *"Geronimo!"* I hear voices whisper and I know not to fire. Medics! It's the Medics! I try to tell Carlos that he will be alright, but Carlos is not awake. He hasn't been awake for a long while. "Geronimo!" "Geronimo!" I frantically echo the whispered code word until I signal a medic.

The Corporal stuffs some sort of white powder into Carlo's mouth and forces water past his lips and into his cheeks. He puts one hand under my friend's neck and lifts his head. He pulls at the Adams Apple with the other hand and I hear the liquid mixture bump heavily down Carlo's throat. The "reclaim" detail is on site. Red Cross stretchers and body bags are décor of the evening. I become part of the search-and-rescue team. It's a long night. After a re-issue of k-rations, I go inland with arriving troops. Carlos is hauled off by the Red Cross emergency unit. I don't know if he is alive or dead. I wonder if I will ever see my best buddy again.

The war was over in 1945. I lost my best friend and my left arm, but I made it through. How I made it without Carlos I don't know. I'm glad to be alive.

The V.A. did what they could with my arm and sent me from the hospital back to Abilene. There is a Military Commendations Celebration at Veterans Hall today. This is my first venture out of the house since I got back. I've stayed indoors with my memories and my nightmares. The nightmares that wake me up screaming, every night, just before dawn.

I enter the Hall and the first person I see is Charlie Sosa. He's looking right at me with that same old evil look in his eye. He's got two goons with him, one on each side. "Here comes trouble," I think as Charlie and his goons stare across the floor in my direction. "That flat, ugly face is as sinister and disgusting as ever." The emcee makes an announcement into the mic behind me but I don't quite catch it. I keep my eye on Sosa and his boys.

"This ain't third grade," I whisper under my breath as if I'm practicing what I'm going to say to Charlie. Meanwhile, some guy hopping across the floor on one leg and a crutch crosses Charlie's path. My eyes fall on this interruption and – oh my God – it's C.J.

I can't believe it. Carlos Jimenez just hopped across the floor to the refreshment table. He leans against the table, scoops some purple punch into a paper cup, looks at me as if he has been waiting for me to surface, and stretches the cup out at me. I rush to his side. "My God, C.J. I thought you were dead." I take the paper cup from C.J.'s hand. He fills a second cup and we drink a toast to each other. We stand in the middle of the room, propped up by the table, and hug each other as best we can. Tears well up in our eyes.

When we look up Charlie Sosa is near. "Lord, C.J., are you still fighting my battles?" I grin sheepishly. C.J. doesn't have his right leg, so he positions himself to the left of me and steadies his balance. I put down the paper cup. I still have my right arm, I'm right-handed, and I am ready.

With escorts on either side of him, Charlie Sosa approaches, floats past both of us and up to the microphone. Blind! In both eyes!

Charlie Sosa received the Purple Heart that day.

The war is over.

WHEELS

Popping wheelies... Nobody believes I pop wheelies in a motorized wheelchair as I speed down surface streets near my home, the home in which I live alone, paying rent, taking care of my business and myself, without assistance. Nobody believes me capable of independence; but back to my wheels.

Most folks know me as "Wheelie." Wheels have been my legs since Nam. I know how wheels work and I know how to work them. Electric wheels are my dance partners. I lead our band and conduct our ballet. We are precision teamwork! One in grace and flow! There is nothing we can't do together.

A squad car saw me pop a few wheelies on my way to the V.A. one morning. The cop couldn't believe what he saw and I couldn't believe he pulled me over and wrote me a ticket for reckless driving.

I never paid the ticket, of course. Never went to traffic court. I'm handicapped you know. Making it to the Court House constitutes extreme physical hardship for me.

A warrant was issued for my arrest. I ignored it.

In time, the fine increased from two to three digits. I let it slide. It reached four digits.

At four digits a warrant was issued for my arrest.

Then I got the summons...

When I got the summons I got myself a lawyer. And never mind the four digits! My lawyer got me *six* digits in the civil suit against the police department!

I'm handicapped you know.

I'm a wheelie-popping wounded warrior but I reason quite well. Far better than most!

And, more often than not, I smile all the way to the bank.

WHAT IF

What if a song held a civilization captive and we called it a national anthem and we blindly fell into the political pit with the enemies on our own soil and they convinced us that we were in danger if we didn't arm ourselves and defend our culture against terror designed to steal our souls and sell our children down the river to foreign shores?

What if we didn't believe the hype and said so and refused to follow orders to kill or be killed?

What if we just said 'no'?

What if we turned our backs on war and hummed a different tune?

What if we sang a different song?

What?

What if?

VALENTINO

The cane leaned against the wall while he hopped around dancing
to the old doo-wop medleys that we used to sing on the corners
in the old neighborhood on warm evenings before the draft.

He was fun then.
He had a sense of humor that kept the whole neighborhood
alive and alert.

Then they sent him away.
And when he came back his extraordinary smile
was a permanent frown
held together by 80 stitches and reconstructive surgery.

But every now and then
(when the right music plays)
that old man can doo-wop
like he's still got two good legs.

THANKSGIVING

(a living epic in one act)

NOTE:

* **Henry "Box" Brown** was a 19th-century Virginia slave who (after 33 years of slavery) escaped to freedom by climbing into a wooden crate and having himself mailed to Philadelphia where slavery had been abolished.

THANKSGIVING

The characters are years:

2003	scene 1
2004	scene 2
2005	scene 3
2006	scene 4
2007	scene 5
2008	scene 6
etc.	

This is a story of war. War in Iraq, specifically, and of other American war and conflict issues as viewed every year on Thanksgiving Day.

And this is a *living* play in which a character (year) is added every Thanksgiving for as long as the madness of war lasts. Each character (year) gives an account of the war as it is covered by the media on Thanksgiving Day.

Set: Kitchen
        Television set
        Radio

The year, wearing a year-number sash, is in the kitchen preparing Thanksgiving dinner while relaying what he/she is hearing on television and radio.

All interpretive freedom to the director

Scene 1 - 2003

Its Thanksgiving morning. The turkey is in the oven. The dressing waits in a buttered pan because the oven is too small for two items. The sweet taste of winter-wheat bread makes the raw dressing ambrosia to selective taste buds. String beans are freshly snapped, succulent, and crisp; and the creamy potato salad melts in your mouth like sin.

The silence of the morning is broken by jazz piped over clear radio waves. Pictures from Iraq call up prayers of safety along with thanksgiving. The television and radio keep dual vigil on world affairs. Convoy fires and bloodshed outline the military chow line. Turkey and gravy is served on metal trays. The troops take turns eating and standing guard. Eat and stand guard. Eat and stand guard. The enemy neither sleeps nor worships.

Blessed is the man who has no complaints, or, if he does, holds them dear and near to his own heart and pushes a positive countenance forward onto a world of pseudo-sharing and phony caring.

Thoughts of good times, better days, and family affairs at the end of this reign of tyranny lead to wistful thinking. Things are never as the dream. An old agenda won't play out in the *new* Jerusalem.

Thanks for vision. Thanks for wisdom. Thanks for strength and conviction. Thanks for stamina. Thanks for inner gifts that overshadow memory.

The little corner of the room that gets the peaceful reflection from an overcast sun; thanks for that place.

The view of the neighbors' rooftop that obscures the distant landscape and serves up a reality break; thanks for that view. The parameters of the world are too far apart and too isolated to commune with God.

Thanks for a key that fits a door to a place called home. Yesterday's coffee reheats well.

Scene 2 - 2004

The President calls the troops to say thanks.

The faces look too young to die, but they do. The faces of the enemy look the same. Too young to die, but they do.

Lottery winners pull the discarded ticket from trash still standing on a New York street due to the garbage strike. They smile for the camera and renew hope across life's mezzanine. The weather holds its head high above the misery of winter, not ready for a total freeze.

Turkeys cook.

The world looks for reasons.

Thanks. It looks for thanks.

The turkey is done. The meal is over. Now it's time for Christmas. The stores blink their colorful lights.

Sale over here!

Sale over here!

Charge!
Charge!

Buy now, pay later.
Buy now, pay later.

Buy now, pay later.

Scene 3 - 2005

Hillary Clinton meets with Afghanistan President Karzai.

The fires in Iraq blaze on.

The weapons of mass destruction are not there.

City walls crumble and fall to hunger, thirst, and disease.

Bush goes to Baghdad. Allah oversees the landing of Air Force One.

My friends are homeless behind the World-Com/Enron fallout. Dominoes continue to fall. It's the old trickle-down theory.

And what about Xmas?

What will happen once Christ is permanently removed from the equation?

The death toll rises.

Martha Stewart is the new domino.

In the morning we'll have hot coffee, creamed chipped turkey on toast, and we will all give thanks for our 'Shit on a Shingle'.

Scene 4 - 2006

What year is this?

What does it matter, the troops are still there.

Death tends to be permanent.

This is no movie. There is no instant replay. Another year and the death toll rises.

Did I mention the Tsunami?

And what's the latest on Darfur and the Sudan?

What about Afghanistan?

The death toll rises. And London bridges all fall down.

And turkeys are on sale. Buy one get one free.

Thanksgiving is back again.

And the death toll rises.

And the death toll rises.

Scene 5 - 2007

It's thanksgiving 2007. How are the troops celebrating?

Air Force One is not flying. Jena Bush got herself engaged in August and Thanksgiving dinner with the new son-in-law-to-be is the order of the day. Let us all drink to that! And to the procreation of more little bushes for the gods to bless.

But what about the troops? How are they celebrating? It's six a.m. There's nothing on the news. Change the channel.

Perhaps the war is sleeping. Let's wait. Let's wait until after the story of snow machines cranking out fake powder for California slopes. Gotta get those ski resorts open!

The weather is on the chilly side. Proceeds for the 14th annual Run to Feed the Hungry will benefit the Sacramento Food Bank. The menu for Mr. President and his future son-in-law includes Turkey, Sweet Potato Soufflé, and Pumpkin Moose Truffle. Wonder what the troops are having?

New candidates campaign for the White House. Giuliani shakes yet another hand. True or False. The trivia question is whether the Pilgrims took beer with them on their voyage. I say true. I say they called it *mead* at the time. We break for commercial. We sell pies and new hybrid cars. The trivia answer is *true*. No mention of mead, however, just true. Fade to the local food bank and the kid volunteers in bright blue t-shirts. Weather. Traffic. Charity. But what about the troops?

Channel change. Tom Cruise. Celebrity invasion. X-box games. Infomercials. Marie Osmond fainting tapes. "Oil Spill Scandal Building!" Blame the Coast Guard. It's after six a.m. Are the troops up yet? Is the war on hold? Boreal is open. Heavenly opens tomorrow. The President is on his way to Camp David for dinner with future son-in-law, Henry. Flash over to captions of legislative debate about bringing the troops home by December, 2008. Maybe? Flash out. No details. Tune in later. But when?

Traffic problems at 6:06. 6:07: Macy's Parade underway; with new balloons! 81st annual Macy's Thanksgiving Day Parade! Very ugly! Uncovered cars dragging lifeless balloons! No mystery. No magic. No personality. No heart. 6:08: Break for commercial. Break for commercial. Break for commercial.

Global warming attributed to cows. Cow Power! Nothing about our troops. I'd better go cook. Its clear skies and cranberry sauce.

Some cameo spots and a couple of video messages come through at last. These youngsters look scared and stressed. We move to Afghanistan where we find a family named Pruitt who are all together in Afghanistan. Each one in uniform. Each one serving his and her country. Each one in a separate camp just a stones throw away from the other.

Praise Him all blessings, great and small!

It's thanksgiving 2007.

That is all we hear of the troops.

Scene 6 - 2008

Thanksgiving came and went this year with no mention of the war
or the troops.

There was no word.
There was no news.
There was no tribute.
There was no salute.

Nobody went there.
Air Force One didn't fly.
Corporate jets didn't dot the sky.
I guess, politically, there was no reason why.

People die all over the world.
Some by fire.
Some by greed.
Some we simply refuse to feed.

But nobody made the trip this year.
Nobody shed a tear.

Scene 7 - 2009

Not one comment was made on the subject of the war this year even though the situation remains critical.

Well, I guess we should give thanks for a quiet day and a quiet dinner.

Scene 8 - 2010

Thanksgiving passed again this year with no word on the war or the troops. I guess both are old news and there are other issues at the forefront. Let's see...

Well for one:
The bipartisan House Ethics Committee recommended that embattled New York democrat Charles B. Rangel be censured by the full House of Representatives for ethics violations. He didn't pay *all* of his taxes! His penalty of censure is the stiffest an Ethics Committee member can face, short of expulsion.

And two:
Unemployment insurance benefits for qualifying recipients have been discontinued. There is not enough money to repay the newly laid off labor force.

And three:
Tax breaks for corporate America have been extended and are scheduled to increase from $28 million to $100 million and possibly more. Sorry, Labor. You loose again!

And four:
Childcare is discontinued for women in the Welfare-to-Work program. (Next they will take away their children.) Being poor is a crime you know. At least in this country. When the troops come home they'll see. They will see!

God Bless America!

(patriotic music)

Scene 9 - the war is over

The president said: "The war is over and we won."

Yet every day a piece of the future crumbles.

Shot down. Mailed home like Henry "Box" Brown* leaving family and friends to mourn and carry on.

In twenty more years descendants of these slain will replace those slain. That's just how it happens. Today's young widow suckles tomorrow's corpse.

"The war is over and we won!"

"The war is over and we won," while bits and pieces of the future come home in hollow boxes draped with somber stripes and stars. There is no shelter from aggression. It's a diseased world. A world of might makes right. A world that knows no sharing. A world of rape and take. Not a respecter of persons, but mongers of conquer.

A mother's tears can't stop bullets. She tills the soil cautiously but sows her seeds in killing fields.

She prays for life or clean, swift death.

While dangers gather, dried-up old men meet and confer, looking through privilege for someone else to blame.

What?   Where?

Well, where the hell is Afghanistan?

Jeannette DesBoine

Scene 10 - 2011 +

Drum roll.

2011 marches in.

Future years march behind her, single file.

The sound and cadence of marching combat boots is deafening.

2011 looks right and left – says nothing – salutes –
peals off stage right and disappears.

Future years (wearing sashes identifying their year) follow 2011 in
single file from back stage to front center and peal off,
exiting at opposing right and left wings.

2012

2013

etc.

etc.

2016

2017

fade out

Scene 11 - Closing

light/dark
lightening flashes
like bombs

gunfire

war sounds

loud shots continue firing
as
screams of men, women, and children
in
different voices and languages
explode and dwindle to an aggravating and indistinguishable hiss

the players line up to
take their bows

they bow and exit as
sounds of war continue in the background

war sounds continue past curtain
and while the audience files out

THE END?

THE TUBA

the drum rolls
and the man struggling with the tuba
breaks into a sweat...but
he doesn't break stride

keeping step with the times...
he wonders if he marches
to the proper drummer

is the beat he hears
the heartbeat of the hordes
who wander fields
crushing flowers to potpourri

is his step too steep
and the driving beat meant to sterilize thought
until the instrument in his left hand is no longer the tuba
but a weapon of mass destruction

or is the beat he hears
the heartbeat of hordes...
wandering fields...
crushing flowers to potpourri

IN THE BEGINNING

In the beginning there was nothing. Then there was sound. And soon after sound there was movement. And no matter what you say, dance was the first creation on earth. Birds did it. Bees did it. And we all know about fleas and the way they created the jitterbug.

Now we dance as ritual. We don't dance for love. We dance to compete. We dance to prove we are better 'steppers' than the competition. We dance on television and let somebody else (who we never see dancing) judge our dance and tell us whether or not we are any good.

We used to dance for pleasure. For release. For relaxation. Now we dance for money and recognition. In the beginning we held each other gently and glided across space in unison. Then we parted. Pulled away from each other! If the dance space was crowded, we lost our original partners as other dancers infiltrated the deserted space. Soon we danced alone, and by the time we found each other again we found the adagio, the tango, and types of movement which included violence in their interpretation.

We shimmied, we twisted, we jerked. We did the monkey and the snake. We mashed potatoes, did the grind, the bump, and committed other acts of frenzied movement that require knocking each other about.

But in the beginning, we held each other close and whispered in each other's ear. We felt the sweet breath of caring on the backs of our necks.

But as the world became increasingly complicated, so did movement.

And so did sound.

And so did dance.

When did our waltz become bombs bursting air?

And why do our classics bellow?

DIABOLICAL CONSEQUENCES

Julian and his family sit outside in the rain.

This is his reward for the years he has given. Years dedicated to dogma designed to benefit the privileged few. Those in control. Those in power. Those hoarding dollars and doling out despair.

There are many like Julian. Wounded. Psychologically, mentally, physically. Those pitching tents under freeways. Those whose purple hearts are discarded along with all their meager possessions when the police make sweeps, dump property, and reclaim grocery carts.

Julian has a good heart and an open mind.

Julian also has a family that he cannot feed because Julian has no pension for his services.

Now, Julian has PTSD. Post Traumatic Stress Disorder. Not from his days in the military, not from his time in the war zone, not from bombs and missiles but from days and nights on the street, without food, without care, without hope.

Terror is a presidential platform, but peace, an unheard-of concept.

Is peace is a term turned female?

A term only mothers can love?

TRICKS

march to the sound of the major chord. make noises of understanding. mimic mass choirs. stand in line. wait for green lights that signal clear passage to oblivion. no one knows the size of the void behind the open palm.

care is the option. ride the rails. carry thoughts that connect relationships to the vastness of need and dare. it's empty in the boxcars. minds matter not. money floats boats. with no money there is no ride.

swimmers wade in change. afloat on legalese and no-lo-contendre. their mechanical motions click and snap rote like ice caps in the wind. wind-up the dolls. set the sheep out to pasture. point them toward the meadow. call the shepherd home then remove familiar landmarks from the shore.

lost. lost and found. found under rocks. found withering beyond the grave. found lurking in dark shadows. plug in hope and fortune. see the fortunate hit the switch that electrocutes opposition; that fry's dissention to a crisp; that crunches heads, pops pimples, bulges eyes and breaks spirits.

lamps spill coal oil over calloused heels. goldenrod & sweet-grass lead back to the beginning. start over. mark the trail with succulent bread crumbs quickly eaten by mirrors in midnight mass. chaos awaits modern miracle. doors open outward onto mainsprings wound tightly around wrists and reality. manacles settle on the mindless while warriors race mission and objective.

the silence is deafening. the coolness of barren night awaits its unsuspecting prey. those who dream. those whose dreams become prayers earnestly offered to the god of nightmare and frozen heartbeats.

steam bathes a burnt-out brainstem. there are no doors labeled *exit,* only windmills turning time to tricks.

FIVE

SCENE OF THE CRIME

Pictures are all over everything. Spilling off the table onto the cold tile floor, magnetized onto the door and sides of the refrigerator, push-pinned to dining and living-room walls, and lining every trash can in this place.

A long-legged man with noticeable ear-hair takes notes. The scuffed-up Stacey's with no arch support speak flat-feet. The severely creased linen suit and blood stained Fedora tell the rest.

He writes:

"Her whole life has to be in these pictures. And even with names and data scribbled on the backs of most of the shots, who can guess who all of these faces belong to. After all, what's in a name? Or a date?

[1]Waist length hair tied in knots and coiled around head like crown. [2]Silk scarf (green) twisted around neck - probably incidental to tragedy. [3]Emerald eyes, open, staring at ceiling.

Who wanted her dead? Why? Did assailant find what he looked for? How many photos does she actually have around this place anyway and where were they kept before this mess? Are there copies? Where?"

Eddie, the coroner's aide, sulks in an empty corner, scanning the radio waves while his department waits to remove the body. *"Renowned Bay Area Photographer Found Dead at her Beachfront Property. Angelina Thibodaux Victim of Attack. Details at 10:00."*

Eddie changes the station. The crime-team still isn't done

with its investigation. Eddie plays with the radio and taps his foot in agitated silence. When the foot stops, the knees start. Eddie unconsciously pumps his right knee for a few minutes. Then the left knee, up, down, up, down. When he stops his knees from jerking, he cracks his knuckles, one joint at a time. Pop! Click! Snap! Eddie hates waiting more than he hates the severity of his A.D.D.

Meanwhile, Smoothe Stone of STONE, STONE, AND BLAKE: DETECTIVE AGENCY mills about the scene, getting in everybody's way. How did he get in? Well, you know Stone. He has a way of sliding through crowds by blending in with scenery. He's been known to ooze under a few doors in his time. This time Smoothe slipped in with Special Investigations, Plain Clothes Division.

"How long has she been dead?" Smoothe asks Eddie, jotting down answers and scribbling interrogation notes on a yellow pad until officers recognize that he is out of jurisdiction and the Lieutenant orders him off the premises.

"Sure thing, Chief. I'm leaving right now." These two used to work together, Smoothe and the Lieutenant, but that was before some serious bad blood separated them.

Smoothe shoots Lieutenant Donavicci a sincere look, tips his mangy Fedora and heads for the front door. Just around the first turn, and out of sight, he ducks into the deceased's bedroom and starts searching for whatever he can find. "This room looks like Nam with all this god-awful bamboo wall-paper!" He scribbles this note on his pad. Smoothe Stone is a detail nit-picker.

Smoothe is careful not to disturb the scene in the front rooms or call attention to the fact that he is still on site. He visually sweeps the bedroom area, and seeing nothing out of the ordinary, he opens the door to what turns out to be a deceptively massive walk-in closet.

Smoothe quickly infiltrates the enormous space and silently shuts the door. He switches on the closet light and rambles around for clues.

"Hhmm! What have we here?" At the west end of the closet, behind long, beaded gowns and full length mink coats is an obscure crease in the wall. Smoothe finds it by accident when he positions his hands to more comfortably flip through Angelina's clothes and rifle through her coat pockets. There's a slight rise under a bamboo-shoot. A crease underneath the god-awful wall-paper.

Smoothe slides his hand towards the ceiling and down to the floor and discovers a lump running down the center of the paper covered wall.

"Hey! What is this? And why is it here?"

Being the world's greatest detective (as Smoothe constantly declares to all who will listen) he taps the wall and runs his palm across the wall-paper.

"Hhmm! Hollow! That shouldn't be!" The lumpy seam under the paper reveals a definite indentation. Some sort of notch contrary to basic construction techniques. Smoothe leans into the wall and pushes the rise to the right. The wall slides. A hidden door opens. "Bingo!" Smoothe cautiously lifts one flat foot and plants it on the other side of this secret hole in the middle of the closet.

"My, my. A dark room! Pretty big too!" As Smoothe steps through to the other side he pulls a dangling cord. A subdued red light warms the room. "Well, now!" Smoothe tells himself, "Let's see what we find here!"

The darkroom door closes automatically. And it closes with the suction of a vacuum seal. Stone makes that mental note while he cases the quiet room.

Stone is unusually careful not to touch anything, but there's nothing to touch. No negatives. No drying prints. Nothing that can be ruined, therefore, nothing to stop him from turning on the overhead light. But as he stretches his right hand toward the switch a flash of lightening sets off a blaze of white-fire behind his eyeballs as major pain explodes in his left temple just above his bleeding nose. There is an intense scramble but nobody hears it outside the vacuum-sealed room.

* *

Eddie Lambert is still waiting for the crime team to end their investigation. When they dust and lift the final fingerprint and pop off the latex gloves the lieutenant looks over, heaves a hoarse "That's a wrap!" and gives the coroner the nod to remove the body.

Coroner Clayton makes it official. "Okay," he tells Eddie. "That's a wrap. Let's get this thing done."

Now Eddie is in charge.

"We'll be out of here in less than ten minutes, kid." Eddie whispers, winks, and flirts with Jacqueline Devine, the newest and cutest department recruit. "It'll be over and done in no time and there'll be nothing left in this place but questions."

Nothing, that is, except Smoothe Stone who is struggling with a sudden breach of silence and a figure that leaped from behind a wall of boxes and caught him by surprise. But Smoothe is bigger than his assailant. He can tell because the sucker-punch (delivered with a bottle of some kind) caught Smoothe below the hairline, an indication that the attacker is shorter.

"Hold it, Maggot!" Stone peels the little guy off his neck and whips out his .45 in record time. "Back up! Let me see your hands or I'll blow you into next week! Get back against that wall! Back! Good thing for you I brought along this set of cuffs. Now, maybe I won't have to kill you. Get those hands out here!"

Stone clamps the cuffs on the perpetrator, flips the overhead light-switch with the barrel of his forty-five and slides the secret door to the left. The door pops and slides open. Smoothe screams bloody murder: "Hey! Somebody! Anybody out there? I need some help in here! I think we've got the perp! H E L L O! "

Donavicci leads the rush to the bedroom. All weapons drawn and ready to fire, he, and what seems like the whole 5th Precinct file into the bedroom, drop, and take aim.

"DON'T SHOOT ME YOU IDIOTS! I'm the one who caught the perp! Smoothe Stone! Ace Detective! How you like me so far?"

TO BE CONTINUED…

Tune in again next time

Same Smoothe time

Same Smoothe Station

Find out who was in that dark-room!!!

SUITE 14

Smoothe Stone is on the scene again, bent over the remains of a small man with a hole in his chest and blood pooled under his body.

Stone isn't fidgeting around. Not calling attention to himself as is his normal modus operandi. This time he scribbles notes on a pocket-sized notepad and barely breathes.

"Joe Silverino – shot once in the heart – dead instantly by all indications." The detective accents his notes with audible whispers as he closes the notepad and walks over to the attending coroners' technician.

"A .45 I think." The technician answers Stone's question before Stone has a chance to ask it. Stone looks over the top of his new silver-rimmed bifocals. The tech looks familiar. Stone has seen this guy before...somewhere. The name tag reads: Oliver Westfall.

"What makes you think it was a .45 Oliver?" Stone quizzes as he studies Oliver's face for identity clues. Then it came to him. "Didn't I see you last Tuesday night at the Suite?"

The Suite is a favorite of Stone's. He frequents it often after a hard day's work. Angie Madison mixes a mean drink and she's really easy on Stones' eyes. If he has his way, she'll be the next one he takes home to mama – so to speak.

"I beg your pardon?" Oliver's back goes rigid, making him look taller than his 6'4" frame. He adds a quick "No. Not me." to his response.

Stone reopens his notepad and writes: *Note to self - Tuesday p.m. - Suite 14 - Coroner's Tech and deceased in fight over redheaded female.* Stone barely finishes his notes when visuals of the actual scene fill his head. The technician and the deceased were at the Club fighting over a redheaded woman. The fight ended on a bad note, indicating that the issue was far from over and nowhere near closed. *# Mental note...* Stone scribbles the hash tag in the margins of the pad and further accents his notes with quickly crafted stars: ***

Detective Stone takes a quick survey of the onlookers at the scene of the crime. A red-headed woman cowers in the shadows at the back of the crowd.

Stone beckons to Sgt. Cooper, his assistant, who rushes right over. "Search this dude," Stone instructs. Cooper frisks the tech. Oliver resists and is restrained by task force agents. Cooper removes a .45 from inside Oliver's smock.

(What stupid sucker is strapped on the job? Dude watches too many movies!) Stone is whispering to himself again.

The gun smells of carbon from recent use, giving Stone cause. "Arrest him," Stone orders, "and don't forget to read him his rights."

Task Force follows through, snapping the cuffs on the coroners' technician and leading him away.

Meanwhile, the red-headed woman has disappeared.

But Stone knows where to find her. He heads for Suite 14.

TRIANGLE

As our story unfolds, LaKreisha is cleaning the kitchen from last night's meal. She hums one of those "nothing tunes" under her breath. She calls them nothing tunes because they're just little tunes that she makes up in the moment. She does this a lot, makes noises to entertain herself and pass the time.

As she works in the kitchen, her mind drifts to last night when he came home with blood on his hands and powder on his shoes. A chalk-white powder like Plaster-of-Paris before it gets wet and sets. She remembers how she looked into his eyes and waited. Waited for word, waited for explanation, waited for a story, a reason for his being so disheveled. No words were offered up. She said nothing.

He went into the bathroom. She listened to the water run until a crisp splash indicated that he had climbed into the tub. He bathed himself for an unusually long time. She turned up the heat. It was growing cold; dark. She lit a candle, said a little prayer, and went to the kitchen to fix his dinner. She had a special meal planned for tonight.

When he finally came to the table they ate in silence. He loved spicy foods and she watched him eat the highly seasoned meal she had prepared for him. And she watched the eyes across the table. Eyes full of warning. Eyes warning her not to speak. Eyes promising to deal with her later. She concentrated on those eyes and thought about running, but decided against it. She kept quiet and watched him eat. He bolted the food and glared at her, but he ate well. He had an almost ravenous appetite for such a small man. He always did. And she always made sure he had plenty to eat. She thought she saw tears in his eyes when he finally got up from the table.

He went into the bedroom. She made no effort to follow even though he left the door open. She stayed at the table and sipped her coffee, which was now cold and tasteless. She could hear him whimpering. She sat perfectly still and listened as his sobs began to saturate the silent night. She hummed very softly to herself, not wanting to disturb him. When she could barely hear him anymore she exhaled and her hum grew more relaxed. She faded into the moment, reflecting on her life with him.

Elton was his best friend. They were children together, grew up together like brothers, always there for each other, lifelong buddies.

But Elton was her friend too. He was the best friend she had ever had. Over time, something special grew between them. He was always there for her. He was there whenever she needed him most. There when she had to run and hide. There when she suffered and healed. There when she lost little Bobby. There when she refused his advice and returned to that distraught house. Yes, he was her friend, but she knew he was gone now. She knew he was dead and buried under enough concrete to conceal his grave forever. No prying eyes or preying animals would ever find him. She wiped her eyes, sat rigidly, and gazed into space; humming a steady stream of dark notes and broken chords. *Hmm hm hmm mm hmhm*. A nothing tune.

When the morning sun peaked through the kitchen window LaKreisha got up, crossed the dining room and closed the bedroom door. She returned to the kitchen and turned on the radio. She switched the dial from his favorite station to her favorite station. *"He always owned that radio!"* Her thoughts were everywhere.

She returned to tasks at hand, restacked her special spice rack and put it away, cleared the dinner table, sterilized last night's dishes in Clorox and boiling water while she listened to HIS radio. *"A time to reap. A time to sow."* LaKreisha always loved this song. She hummed under her breath. This was no nothing tune. This was the Byrds.

The urge to run picked at LaKreisha's last nerve, but she quickly dismissed the image. "It's over! There'll be no more running," she insisted. The sound of her voice startled her. "He will never put his filthy hands on me again."

LaKreisha looked at the phone for a while, then finally picked it up and dialed 911. As the phone rang she tuned into the sound of the music. *For every season...* "I know this part!" She congratulated herself and edged her raspy voice in with the chorus of *turn, turn, turn, turn.* Confidence amplified her volume and she lost herself in the tune. She was singing lead with the Byrds when police dispatch picked up the phone and put her on hold. *There is a reason... turn, turn, turn, turn.* LaKreisha increased the radio's volume. She knew this part well. She sang with abandon.

> *A time to reap -*
> *A time to sow -*
> *A time to plant -*
> *A time to pull up what is planted....*

OPENING NIGHT

Music was all she had left and she certainly was enjoying it. It was her anniversary and they were going to Vegas. She was excited about the trip and let herself forget certain little quirks of his personality. She ignored the new stripes on her flesh. The stripes he put there and would add to whenever he felt depressed and unsure of himself.

There were many things he took out on her. He could strike without warning and she often found herself on the receiving end of misery. But this was their anniversary. She only wanted to think of good times. If she searched long and deep enough, certainly she could find some good times to remember. This trip would be good. It was seven years since they had planned a trip together. She held the tickets in her hand. This trip was going to make a difference. It would be the turning point in her life. She would to see to that. She had made plans. This was going to be her happiest anniversary ever.

He was in good spirits the day before the plane was to take off from Phoenix to Vegas. He talked to her practically all night about his love for her and about his past mistakes. He apologized profusely for bygone wrongs. Of course, he never meant any of things that he had done and it would never happen again. He was going to get help. He would do therapy. They could do therapy together, he suggested. "I love you more than my next breath." He swore to it, and repeated it over and over as if he were trying to convince himself. She had heard it all before, but she wanted to believe. She held him, reassuring him of her forgiveness and of her unconditional love. "Vegas here we come," they wailed in harmony as they fell into each other's arms and fell asleep giggling about the trip.

The sun came early. The bags were already at the front door. She flipped the switch on the coffee maker and their coffee was ready in less than a minute. They only had time for a quick cup while they gathered themselves together and waited for the cab. He had pre-arranged all the details. He liked controlling everything and she had to let him. There was a 'toot-toot' from outside. The cab driver backed the cab into the driveway. Lee grabbed the two bags and took them out while she pulled the plug on the coffee pot, turned off the lights, and locked the door. She gave Lee his keys as they climbed into the back of the cab. She looked at him and smiled.

They were at the airport in no time. The freeway was clear. Who else would be up and on the road at such an ungodly hour? The sun was just tipping its hat to the moon, but she was not complaining. After all, this was her anniversary and she planned to enjoy every second of it. She even had rolls of pennies in her suitcase in case all else failed. Oh yes, she had plans, and she deserved this vacation. She had earned it. It was her reward. Reparations! A celebration. A fling. Her chance to walk the wild side...

They boarded the plane. She stood behind him and waited as he sank into seat C, the window seat. The middle seat was never her favorite. In fact, she hated the middle seat with a passion, but she crawled in and tried to find room to rest her elbows, a problem exacerbated when the aisle seat filled with the body of a huge man with a black beard and the smell of Aramis. She scrunched in between the two men. It was an easy take off and an easy ride in spite of the conversation between her husband and his newly-found traveling companion. They ordered drinks and struck up a friendship. She had tea. The men's raucous conversation ricocheted off her tea cup and bounced off her magazine. She tried to concentrate on an article about Oprah.

Their traveling companion was Oscar. A musician gigging in Vegas. They'll check out his show. Oh, they're staying in the same hotel. What a coincidence. Their conversation bounced back and forth as if Sheila wasn't there.

"It's her anniversary." The words aimed at Oscar trimmed her right ear. "What're you gonna do? You know women!" A chuckle slid past her left ear this time. "Indeed I do," Oscar replied. She and Oscar exchanged a glance.

The fellas laughed at each other's knowledge of women and chugged down their drinks just as the stewardess held out the plastic garbage bag. Lee lobbed his cup into the bag. "Two points," he proclaimed proudly. Sheila wadded up her napkin, put it and the teacup into Oscar's big hand. She watched him drop the items into the trash. Her left eye twitched. They fastened their seat belts and assumed landing position.

"Vegas," Sheila whispered and sighed.

Oscar and Lee were saying goodbye as she flagged down a cab. Lee threw the bags in the trunk and flopped down in the back seat. She watched his eyes and searched his face for remnants of last night's celebration. There were no signs. She left it alone. They rode to the hotel in silence.

The cabby collected eleven-seventy-five from Lee who grabbed the bags and headed for the hotel doors. Her eyes brightened at the sounds, and the lights, and the noises of the people in the hotel lobby. People who were everywhere and were oblivious of other people around them. Wow! Vegas! Her face broke into smile. She couldn't close her mouth. "This is going to be great," she whispered. "I deserve this."

Lee was at the front desk when she caught up with him. The bell captain had the luggage on rack and two room keys in his hand. The glass elevator floated up the side of the hotel wall. You could see everywhere. She took it all in. She inhaled the lights and the noise. She looked at him as the elevator stopped on the 12th floor. 1217 was the room number. Lee took both the room keys. He opened the door. The bell captain down-loaded the bags, got his tip, and left the two of them alone.

She felt like a kid again! She threw her coat on the bed and grabbed her purse. He had given her a few dollars and she couldn't wait to go look around. He was pouring himself a drink. She felt his mood. She put her purse down, sat on the bed and waited for him to speak. It was eight o'clock in the morning. She had time. As a matter of fact, she had all weekend. This was their anniversary!

Sheila took a deep breath and tried to relax. She tuned into Lee's new mood and acted accordingly.

She was climbing out of the shower when she heard him calling. "Sheila," he yelled. *What now?"* she whispered under her breath. She inhaled and held onto the captured air. She had stayed out of his way on purpose. She didn't even turn her music on because she knew it would give him reason to complain. "Be right there," she answered as she dropped her towel and hurriedly tied the terry cloth robe around her dripping body. "NOW!" he demanded.

Sheila went into the room - ready. He had that look. She saw the slap coming but she didn't try to get out of the way this time. She stretched out her hand and knocked the phone off the hook. Room service would automatically answer. She let him yell his head off. She raised her arms to protect her head. "No, Lee," she kept screaming. "Please! No! Don't jump Lee. Please don't jump." She yelled louder and louder as she manipulated herself into position. She pulled the phone cord until the wires broke loose from the wall. When the phone cords broke loose she stopped yelling.

It was like a rerun. Déjà-vu! Sheila had seen all this before. She co-wrote this script and knew exactly what to expect. This was no dress rehearsal, this was opening night.

There was one loud knock on the door and a deep male voice called Lee's name. The door opened and the voice was instantly inside the room herding Lee furiously toward the balcony.

Lee was no match for the big man from Phoenix. Oscar was in, out, and on his way before Lee knew what hit him.

BACK TO ATHENS

In Greece the weather is mild and rainy in winter, relatively warm and dry in summer, with extended periods of sunshine throughout most of the year. Ivan Constantine arrived in New York just as the weather was transforming from brisk fall to frigid winter. *"It is cold in this place."* Ivan practiced his English. He knew English pretty well.

When Greek economy took a tailspin, Constantine left Greece looking for work. Olive trees could no longer support Ivan's habits of eating and living indoors, so he pulled up stakes, packed a flight bag, and pocketed what little money he had left after he paid for the one-way ticket to New York. He had no idea what he would do in the United States but he had high hopes about survival, after all, he was able-bodied and wise. Ivan also had a habit of talking to himself. *"Is only way to get intelligent conversation,"* he told everybody who ragged him about it.

Walmart gave Ivan his start. He hired on as a Greeter. Low pay, no benefits, but an income of sorts.

Salvation Army Residence Hall provided lodging for the new resident, and when Ivan wasn't working, he ate in their soup kitchen. When he was greeting, which was most of the time, his minimum wages afforded him just enough fast food money for that survival he talked to himself about. *"Is a start!"* he told his reflection as he shaved his face and prepared for work that first morning. *"Is start, Ivan!* he said. *Is start!"*

The few clothes Constantine brought from Athens worked

for him until temperatures in New York grew cold, colder, and in a few weeks, bottomed out. *"My gods,"* Ivan asked himself, *"how cold is going to get this place? It is normal?"*

"Thank gods for Salvation Army." Ivan told the cashier as he paid for a gently used winter coat, snug boots, and a wool ski cap he found in the men's department. He shoved the goods into the canvas tote bag his baby sister had embroidered for him on his 30th birthday. The royal purple and dark red silk read: IVANS STUFF. It was an old joke between the two of them.

Ivan called the Salvation Army store *Sally's,* and when people asked him where he got his things, he would say, *"I got at Sally's"* and smile. If they inquired further he told them *Sally's* was in Harlem, knowing that just the mention of Harlem would end all conversation. *"People so stupid."* The subway was full of people who thought he was talking to them. "Yeah!" commuters near him responded in attempt to initiate conversation. But Ivan was talking to himself, and when he didn't answer the commuters, they eyed him queerly, shrugged their shoulders, and let him alone.

Back in his room he surveyed his new treasures. *"One man's trash is other man's treasure, 'eh Ivan."* His new coat, a black wool military pea-coat, was in excellent condition except for a small round hole in the left breast pocket. The stain around the hole was confined to the inside, but because the coat was such a deep black in color and the fabric such a heavy wool it was almost impossible to see the maroon colored stain. As for the hole, Ivan began another open conversation with himself. *"I can fix! On outside I put pin. Hmm. Lets see. Okay. Here is perfect pin. American Flag. What you think, Ivan? I got him from front desk downstair. Yep. Perfect fit. And nobody will be look inside for anything so little stain be between you and me coat, eh? Deal? Good deal!"*

Ivan placed the pin strategically over the hole and held the coat before the mirror, testing the view as it would be seen from other eyes. The flag concealed the flaw. He shoved his short arms into the coat. *"How I look, eh?"* With his hands in the pockets, Ivan turned side to side and back to front checking himself in the long glass. *"Work for me."* He was getting pretty good at New York slang. He took the coat off and hung it on a wooden hanger; the proper hanger for quality, heavyweight wool. *"Heavy enough for snow and subzero temperature. Not bad for $7.99 Ivan, my boy! Ivan know quality,"* he said proudly. *"I not always been broke."*

Smoothing the lapels and collar, Ivan draped the pea-coat over the hanger and checked the inner pockets to make sure the linings lay flat and weren't all bunched up. *"Oho...what is this here?* From the right breast pocket Ivan recognized a lottery ticket. *"So-o-o!"* he said as he checked the date. It was from August. *"Old. Outdated."* He read the numbers anyway. No big deal. His eyes were getting heavy. Feeling a little weary, he dropped the ticket into his footlocker, snapped the lock and went to sleep. He had long days scheduled all the rest of his work week. He needed his sleep.

On November 6, it started to snow. *"Go ahead and snow you monster! I got good coat and good winter boots. I ready for you!"* It was Friday morning. Ivan had earned a day off by putting in excessive overtime. *"Work enough double shift and get day off just before collapse yourself from exhaustion. Is company policy."* Ivan laughed at his own joke. He had no big plans for the day so he decided to take a walk around the block. Stop in the sports bar down the street. Watch the game. Meet people. This grew to be routine when Ivan wasn't at work. He fashioned himself a social life.

Eventually, Ivan met the woman of his dreams. Priscilla

Pappas; beautiful and Greek. Also from Athens. When Ivan finally convinced her to go out with him he forgot about everything except having enough money to build a relationship her. He was wild about Priscilla. When Priscilla started talking futures, her conversation worried Ivan. *"What sort of future can Walmart job provide?"* He worried about long term plans every time they ate at McDonalds. Somehow, Mickey D's just didn't fit the bill. Ivan really started talking to himself then. *"Champagne taste! McDonald budget! What we will do?"*

"Wonder what Priss is doing. Better call her up. Maybe we get together later. I got enough change to spring for Pizza." It was December 17. Ivan had a pizza coupon that didn't expire until December 23rd. Yes, Ivan was a frugal man and a coupon clipper. He dug around in the footlocker for the pizza coupon and came across the old lotto ticket while he was scrounging around. He had forgotten about that ticket. He pulled it out. *"It's storming out there!"* he told himself. In spite of the snow, he put the coupon and the ticket in his pocket, gathered his wits about him, buttoned his coat to the ears, pulled on his ski cap, and stepped out into the weather. It was no longer snowing, but the cold took Ivan's breath away. He dialed Priscilla's cell phone while he walked the short blocks to Casey's Place. He let Priscilla's phone ring ten times. *"No answer. I try later."*

When Ivan got to Casey's, Priscilla was there, but her phone was at home. He climbed out of his coat and sat with her. They laughed and talked until Ivan remembered the coupon and invited Priss for pizza. The coupon was for Casey's and they only had to walk to the next room to order. When Ivan pulled the coupon from his pocket the lotto ticket came with it. Priss scooped up both items. The coupon covered her favorite pizza. And the ticket? "This ticket is still good," she told Ivan. "It's good for six months. Let's check the numbers." There was a lotto kiosk at the front of Casey's. Priss took the ticket and went to check while Ivan sat at the table checking his change to make sure he had enough to cover the incidental costs that go along with his buy-one-get-one-half-off pizza coupon.

He saw Prissy beckoning him so he put his change in his pocket and joined her at the kiosk. She was pale and stammering. "Read the numbers, Ivan. Read the numbers." She didn't turn the ticket loose, however. She held it so he could see and read its numbers while she verified each one with the print-out in her other hand. Ivan had the winning ticket. Six for six. $3,859,543.00. BAM!!

On New Years Eve, Mr. and Mrs. Ivan Constantine returned to Greece. First class. No luggage. Just the canvas bag with the royal purple and dark red silk letters that spelled out: IVANS STUFF.

It was a new joke between the two of them.

ANOTHER DREAM

Cut to the chase. To a dream of houses with doors that cannot be locked and cellars and attics that have no entry. Closed in. Trapped. Trapped in the magnificence of a turn of the century Victorian amid modern structures where strangers lurk the grounds, peeping through windows that won't close and doors that won't open.

The houses are huge, with many rooms, but no privacy. The world runs amuck around the property. There are children looking in the windows. *What do they want?* They are menacing little monsters who will not go away. They are disrespectful little skin-headed delinquents, out without supervision.

In dream scene two the little monsters get themselves hurt playing on abandoned cars which slip and slide and crash into church walls. Parents show up. They are pseudo neo-nazis who harass and menace. Police are called but do not come.

The doors and windows of the house do not seal. The house is too big to get to all the windows and doors in attempt to secure them. A black child shows up selling a watch. He gets lost in the house, is discovered later and asked to leave. More black males show up. The little skin-headed felons somehow turn protective.

Black girls in theatrical uniforms begin precision dancing. They are quite good. *Now* the police come! They tell the girls: "We don't like what you niggras are doing." This mob; this rioting squad of police; rustles the girls and boys into paddy wagons to haul them off to jail. They don't hear the protests coming from the house. No. They hear but ignore the protests coming from the house. They hear but do not heed.

The children are being roughed-up in the round-up. There is a scuffle. During the scuffling the scene fades to black and I am suddenly awake, cold and trembling.

I have lived this dream before.

GRACE

Ginger tea and lemon bars

Ice cream treats and bumper cars

Pulling teeth and biting nails

Fielding flies and setting sail

Waiting calmly at the beach

Rushing wildly through the streets

Dancing in a chorus line

Talking with two friends of mine

Arch your back and tilt your head

Get the gist of what is said

Pay attention to the score

You can't afford to lose much more

Tell a joke and crack a smile

Give an inch and gain a mile

SIX

OPEN

from nowhere comes that drum
rhythm and sound
movement
dance
spinning words
words hidden behind thought
in tune with cracked and mended chords

rhythm pounding on doors
doorways opening to flooded emotions
hearts in tune with the poetry of children
a child's mind
pure and innocent
whispering
whistling
humming happily at reason
for no reason other than the act of being
being alive
being free
being independent and unmarked by masks
masking nothing nor having need to hide

open
pure
clear and clean
open to wonder and wisdom
led by trust and belief
having faith that only the inner child in all of us enjoys

SQUEAKY

Squeaky is a toad-frog. And although he thinks he is the best thing that has ever happened to the Fraternity of Frogdom, he is ordinary. Just an ordinary run-of-the-mill jerk-legged toad with a big mouth and a horrendous case of Greenwartitis, an incurable skin disease brought on by swimming in slime.

Squeaky thrives on slime. He makes his bed in impure slime. Squeaky thinks slime is a matter of class and breeding. Squeaky is the dumbest frog I have ever met. Oh yes, we've met! I've got the scars to prove it!

Stuck-up and stupid, that's Squeaky. Always name-dropping and talking about how much he paid for everything like he is so *above* the rest of his species. I can't stand him! He's a common amphibian with a life span of ten to twelve years (far too long in my opinion) but, if you let *him* tell it, he is eternal - and that ten to twelve years doesn't apply to him because he's a direct descendant of the Proto-Frog of ancient Madagascar. *Oh, please!*

The origin of the Proto-frog goes back two hundred and sixty five million years. Back to the age of the Permian, who Squeaky claims as his ancestor. Humph! Squeaky is no Permian! Permian lived in fresh water and on dry land. Their skin was slick and glandular, with secretions ranging from distasteful to toxic. Squeaky is just plain warty and couldn't conjure up a secretion if his life depended on it, let alone a toxic secretion. Warty species of frog tend to be called toads. Squeaky is a TOAD! A common, low-class, ill-bred TOAD! He is trash. A tramp. An ugly tramp with

with a taste for goldfish. That's me!

You want to know why I hate Squeaky? Well, duh! Because he keeps trying to eat me that's why! He's eaten plenty of my relatives.

He got mom in '78 and dad in the winter of the same year.

My brother swam his heart out trying to escape captivity, but he ended up a Squeaky sandwich even though he was the strongest swimmer in the family.

Not only do I hate Squeaky, but I hate the stupid humans who come into Jake's Pet Emporium to buy sacks of goldfish to take to their backyard slime-ponds to feed the freaking frogs. Jeez! Mind your own business why don't ya' and leave me and my family alone.

Uh oh! Watch out!

LOOK OUT SIS! HERE HE COMES AGAIN...

SWIM!

SWIM!

SWIM Lilly!

SWIM!!

THE RHINOCEROS AND THE POLKA-DOT PILLOW
(another story for the young at heart)

I wish I could sit on a polka-dot pillow, under a really wide umbrella, next to a gigantic rhinoceros.

It would be like a fairy tale where the rhino is a mythological, magical creature, descendant from kings and queens, and sent to guide and protect me from all sorts of ills. How cool is that?

When we are together, that rhino and me, we will eat whatever Rhinoceroses eat and drink whatever Rhinoceroses drink.

We'll sit in the shade and play games, like Masquerade, where we each pretend to be something that we are not.

On really hot summer days I'll paint the Rhinocerosesesa toe nails. I hope she likes orange. Or maybe pink. Red, I think, is much too brash for a chubby Rhino. And black is too gothic and bone-chilling for a Rhino of any size.

We'll play cards, my Rhino and me, like double Solitaire. I'll let her win a few hands to keep her interested in the game. If she gets bored we can play Chinese Checkers if she can find a way to hold on to her marbles.

I'll name my rhinoceros Rena! I hope she's a nice Rhino. With a sweet disposition. And I hope she can swim close to the surface in deep water so I can ride her back and not get sucked underwater and drown. I never learned to swim you know!

I wish I was a Rhinoceros too! Then Rena and I could compete with one another. See who's the fastest swimmer! Who can hold her breath the longest! Who can eat and drink the most of whatever Rhinoceroseseses eat and drink. That would be fun.

I wonder how we would tell which one of us was the cutest. How would we judge? Maybe we could sit at the edge of the river and wait for some boy type Rhinoceroseseses to come along and we could ask them to judge. Yeah! A Rhino beauty contest. The winner gets a crown of frog legs, fish lips, and fly eyes! *WHOA Buddy!* I wonder what we would wear for the pageant. A bathing suit? (One or two piece?) A tu-tu and ballet slippers? (Who makes slippers that large?) Maybe we could pose in the all-together after we polish up our Rhino hides and clear away all the leaves, mud, and muck.

I wish I could take my Rhinoceros friend home with me. She could sleep in my room. I have bunk beds. She could have the extra bed. I'll take the top bunk and let her have the lower one just to be safe, instead of sorry.

I wonder if I could hide her from Mommy. I don't think Mommy would take to Rena. Especially Rena in a bunk bed. Mommy is just not too keen on animals. She screamed and hid in the closet all day when Tweets got out of her cage. Tweets is just an itsy-bitsy, teeny-weeny little canary bird. Tweets wouldn't hurt a fly.

I wish I lived at the zoo. The zoo has plenty of room for Rena and me. The zoo has special camp sites, and we (Rena and me) why, we could spread out and run around until evening when the shade comes out and its story-telling time.

My Rhinoceros likes story-telling time. I read to her every shady evening. I wish she would read to me too, but she refuses to wear the glasses I gave her for her last birthday. Rena is so vain about her appearance that sometimes she makes me sick! Just plain sick!

You know, sometimes I forget that Rena is not a real Rhinoceros. But I know she could be if she would just read what I write in the dirt. I write her name there all the time. Those glasses look great on her. If only she would wear them and use them to read her own name in the special dirt. If you find your name in the dirt and read it out loud, magic things happen.

Instead, Rena's big, clumsy, near-sighted self stumbles around until she trips over the polka-dot pillow; knocks the wide umbrella all the way across Shallow River Falls; and finally, she trudges back and forth on the enchanted dirt until her big Rhinoceros thighs rub out every last letter of her name.

Oh Rena! For goodness sake!

THE HOMELESS CAT
(a children's story)

Once upon a time there was a cat. A Persian cat. A gray Persian cat with long, spiked hair and a very flat face. This cat lived in San Francisco, on Geary Street near Kearny, close to the A440 Gallery, which was featuring new works by **Mr. Leon Kennedy**, a famous folk-artist who has works in the Smithsonian Institute. That was our destination that Saturday morning when Shawn, my five-year-old companion, and I saw the cat curled up on the sidewalk among the homeless. After considering the situation for what seemed like a long time, Shawn looked up and whispered: "Is that cat homeless? I've never seen a homeless cat before." "Neither have I, Shawn," I confided. We tried not to stare. We didn't want to appear rude.

The cat had a spot in the middle of the many panhandlers and other street-dwellers on Geary Street. A throw-pillow was propped neatly against the wall of one of the high-rise buildings. The cat's body curled around in a circle. He was curled up on the pillow with his head resting on his front paws and his eyes pointing down towards the sidewalk.

This cat's body was unnaturally long. Much too long and far too thin for his breed. Persians are bigger than that, normally. The fur on this cat's body was thinner than the fur on his face and tail. He looked scraggily, like he wasn't eating much and his health was suffering. "Poor Kitty," Shawn said out loud, talking mainly to himself.

Kitty had a tin cup on the sidewalk to the left of his pillow.

I thought it strange that his head faced the other direction. I thought he should be watching his cup. Watching the money he was collecting from generous strangers. There were lots of nickels and dimes in the bottom of that cup.

Yet another stranger walked by and dropped a quarter into the cup. "Ping!" the cup rang out. The cat didn't move. Didn't move an inch! It just lay there with its head facing the concrete. People walked up and down and back and forth in front of the cat but he never moved or acknowledged their presence. He never uttered a "thank you" meow to anyone who dropped coins into his cup, but I know he must have been grateful. He was so very thin! So skinny! His body was so long it looked like a rope. He probably got that way from hunger.

"He looks hungry", Shawn whispered in my ear like he was reading my mind. All I could do was nod my head.

I wanted to ask the cat how long he had been homeless and how he had come to be homeless in the first place, but I didn't ask because he was asleep. Fast asleep! Sleeping like a baby! I didn't dare wake him. He looked like he really needed that sleep.

I wanted to know how long and how far he had traveled to get to this spot. Geary Street in San Francisco seems like the end of the world sometimes, depending on the traffic. I kept watching him sleeping and I began to imagine the amazing stories that this cat had to tell.

Judging by the scar over his left eye (which closed in a strange way because of that scar) well, judging from the way that eye closed, I'll just bet you he used to live on the sea. Shawn and I talked about it and we both figured Kitty for a sea-cat! A pirate! A pirate cat traveling the high-seas in search of adventure. Coast to coast! Continent to continent! He got that scar in a fight with a huge ocean-going rodent; a big fat rat; a dock-rat fighting over the rights to a freshly caught fish. A big, red, fresh, sweet, deep sea Rock Cod! (Now, that's good eating!) The rat got a good lick in, right above that left eye, but the Persian slapped the rat with those razor sharp claws and the rat ran away so he could live to fight another day.

Yeah! This cat had plenty of adventures like that. And plenty of stories to tell, Shawn and I were sure of that.

He wasn't such a young cat. You could tell by the snow-white whiskers surrounding his puffed-up lips. He was sleeping so soundly in the sun that Shawn and I began to wonder if he would ever wake up. One thing about it, whenever he did wake up he would have a lot of change in his cup. Shawn put in the dollar bill he'd been saving in case he saw something he wanted to buy from one of the street vendors. When Kitty woke up he might just have enough money to get himself a room in a nearby hotel and a rich meal full of fresh fish and thick, juicy cream. *Yummy!*

Shawn watched as I dropped my change into the cup, then we said a little prayer for the cat's future. We had never seen a homeless cat before, and we wanted him to be alright so we asked St. Francis, the patron saint of animals, to give him enough cash to get himself off the street before the weather changed from sunny to cold. Enough to get back out to sea where he could live happily ever after.

Finally, Shawn and I made our way to the Gallery to enjoy the artworks of Leon Kennedy. We told Mr. Kennedy about our experiences and Mr. Kennedy sympathized and shared encouraging words of hope with us.

After that, my young friend and I back-tracked quietly through the streets of San Francisco, making our way to the Montgomery Street BART Station where we could catch the train back to Oakland; both of us still thinking about how we had never seen a homeless cat before.

BOY AND DOG

The door opened and the lights came on automatically. "Who's in there?" a dark voice called. But there was no answer.

Heavy footsteps stomped across the wooden floor. Where they came from is a mystery, as is any reputable witness to this adventure.

Three timid mice huddled in the corner of the kitchen. They couldn't run under the stove because the oven was on and the temperature had to be at least 500 degrees.

A skirt flowed across the middle of the kitchen floor. Behind that skirt scurried four fuzzy feet. THE CAT!!! The mice froze to the spot in the corner and listened as the purring came closer and closer. "What will we do?"

All of a sudden the back door flew open. It was Boy and Dog.

Dog went after the cat and chased it into the front bedroom where it was cornered on top of the dresser, the highest point it could find. Dog kept jumping up, but he couldn't reach Cat.

Boy thought these mice he had found frozen to the corner of the kitchen floor belonged to him, like the hamsters in the cage in his room. While The Lady of the Hot Kitchen screamed and fell over in a clump, Boy picked up his mice and took them outside to the secret fort he was building for the Bill and Charlie Wars, which would start as soon as he saw those big bullies coming down the alley past the Chinaberry tree.

He had his weapons and his army in place. He, the General; Dog, the lookout; a brand new sling shot; a bucket full of rock-hard chinaberry bullets; and now his ultimate secret weapon: three petrified mice (the Private, the Corporal, and the Master Sgt.) all on choke-chains.

"Come on Bill and Charlie! I've got you now! Come on!"

THE SUM OF ITS PARTS

Characters:

(LL = left leg & ME = me)

***

LL:

You know, you need to sit yourself down.

ME:

And you need to leave me alone and try to cooperate.
Help me out here! I've got things to do.
Places to go!

LL:

Give me a break will you. Can't you see you're killing me!

ME:

Oh, Pu-leese!

LL:

Oh, please nothing!
Every time you move the Hip burns like wildfire.

ME:

I know.
You rub your bones against each other,
and I don't know why you keep doing that, you idiot!

LL:

Me? It's not me!

ME:

Who is it then?

LL:

You're the one who doesn't take care of your body.
Didn't the doctor tell you to exercise?

ME:

I DO EXERCISE!
I'm trying to exercise right now but you won't cooperate.
Every time I move, you hurt!

LL:

Yeah! I hurt! I have parts! Parts that need tender loving care. TLC!
You know what I mean?

ME:

Listen, Lefty! You *are* a part. I'm the "full-package" around here.
Get over yourself why don't you!

LL:

I'll tell you what. Every time you don't listen, I and my parts, we're going to send you messages. Those messages are called PAIN. Don't play with us! We are all-powerful!

ME:

Look, what do you want from me?
I take you out everyday. I walk you. I rub you down with the best liniment on the market, and still you complain.

LL:

The doctor said swim!
Is that not what the doctor said?

ME:

Yes, that **is** what the doctor said! But like I told the doctor, swimming won't happen. Don't you remember when I tried to teach you how to swim? Remember what you did? You refused to learn! You **and** your precious PARTS!

LL:

What the devil are you talking about?
I don't remember any swimming lessons.

ME:

Oh, yes you do! You and your parts acted a fool!

Ankle twisted. Shin Bone cracked and gave Calf Muscles a
throbbing cramp. Knee popped out of joint.
Hip Bone separated and danced some sort of jig with Tail Bone.
You gonna tell me you don't remember that?

LL:

Well, now that you mention it...
But as far as doctors orders are concerned,
you are out of compliance.

ME:

Look you! I've got something for you and *all* your parts.

LL:

And just what might that be Mz. Full-Package?!

ME:

Pain pills, Lefty! You keep messing with me and you won't even
get a walk. I'll douse you so full of pain medication you won't
know what hit you. I'll medicate until I forget that you and your
hurting parts exist.

LL:

I don't advise you to do that "Full-Package."
That medication only lasts a short while, then it wears off.
We'll get you in your sleep.
Don't mess with us!
Don't you even try it!

Flashbacks!

ME:

Are you threatening me?

LL:

What do you think? Is it a threat? Do you think it's a threat?

ME:

You don't scare me! I can take your little mess. You know why?
Because I have "MIND" on my side. Mind completes me. Mind is
part of the "full-package." Your little parts don't matter. Get it?
Mind over Matter!

LL:

Humph! I hope you hold that thought when Hip Bone jerks a knot
in your pelvic joint. Joints matter. And joints are on *my* side.
Go ahead. Get your meds ready. See what happens. See which of
us is stronger. Pain or your so-called pain-killers.
Pain killers! That's a laugh!
Your pain ain't dead!

Heheheeheehee Aha aha Hahahaahaha! AA Ahhaaa

ME:

OOOO! I HATE YOU!

LL:

Yes, I know.

.

THE LIFEGUARD

I still can't swim, even though my brother, the Lifeguard, said he would teach me.

His lesson consisted of having one of his teenaged classmates help throw me into the deep end of the community pool where the water was ten feet deep then yelling *"swim, swim"* while making swimming motions in the air, waving his arms like a moron while I was going down for the third time.

Oh sure, he pulled me out before my final gasp for air and propped me up on the concrete deck, gagging and spewing anger and fear.

I still can't swim.

I still can't swim and I fear deep water now even more than before.

Well, no, that's not exactly true. I don't fear the deep water as much as I [a] respect all water, and [b] distrust human beings.

A big brother is something special. A big brother is sacred. A big brother is a hero! An idol! A protector almost as strong as a dad! A big brother can do no wrong!

Well, I still can't swim, and I don't dare or care to learn.

The scar tissue that encases that first near-death experience has calcified into the new millennium, but the wound does not heal.

Deeply etched on my soul is the experience itself, along with the awful knowledge that my hero is a moron and my idol is unworthy of trust.

Pick your heroes wisely...

I still can't swim. And I remember that fact ever so vividly every time the lifeguard comes to town!

SEVEN

Jeannette DesBoine

LUNCH DATE

Today I took a real lunch break and went to Subway for the Friday Special: a foot-long Tuna sandwich with chips and a coke. With lunch in tow I drove to Martin Luther King Estuary (an inlet on the Alameda side of the Oakland airport) and parked in a quiet cove where I could watch the water, the birds, and eat in peace.

Birds at the estuary are hard to ignore. I drop a piece of bread out the window and watch a cautious sea-gull tip-toe toward the car, both eyes trained on me as he gobbles up the crust of bread and takes off, immediately airborne. Another gull comes swooping in like a dive bomber and although he missed my first offering, he *(or she, I really don't know which)* raises plenty of hell with the gull that got the goods. I wonder if they are related, you know, like married or something. They argue like people! I tear more bread off my sandwich and throw it onto the black-top, further away from the car. This time, what seems like an entire family of gulls gets in on the dive, although only two or three are successful. Those who don't get a tasty morsel raise hell with the ones who do, screaming, threatening, and even striking out with beaks and wings at the quicker, trickier birds. Their sad behavior is so human!

I remember a box of crackers in back of the car. They've been there, unopened, at least a month. These salt-free mini-crackers sell two boxes for a dollar at Food-for-Less. What a deal! Each box contains two individually wrapped packets the size of large bags of potato chips, but full to the brim, not half empty like the chip bags.

The birds are hungry! I say this to justify my intended actions, but just as soon, I decide that they are simply greedy but I'll feed them anyway. I get out of the car and open the hatch. I figure the gulls will fly away the instant I open the car door, but they hesitate and watch me as if asking: *"Hey, Lady, ya' got any more food!"* They lift off at the noise of the hatch back opening, but they don't go far. They circle the air, getting in a few rounds of exercise. I retrieve my crackers, return to the driver's seat and pry the bag open. *Why do they make stuff so hard to open?* Finally I toss a small handful of salt-free crackers (about six or so) out the window. Lord, you'd think all heaven has broken loose. Gulls come in so fast I can't count them. I swear I saw a one-legged one, but it got lost in the frenzy of the crowd, so I'm not really sure.

This grab and go game continues until lunch time is over and I've got just enough time to drive back to the office without being too visibly late. I crank up the Mariner, lay the cracker bag on the passenger seat where I can get my right hand in as I creep up the narrow road. I reach in the bag and throw out a handful of goodies. Gulls swoop frantically. Like it's a matter of life or death! They dive like kamikazes, trying to beat one another. A few more feet, another handful. Their frenzied movement attracts even more birds. More gulls and other species join the fray. It's a madhouse. Another few feet, another handful. Birds soar and dive but they no longer fight. Fighting would be a waste of time. It would translate to missing a morsel and letting some other lucky duck get more than his share.

Apparently, seagulls are not dumb birds. Every few feet I toss out a new load. My vehicle is now leading Gull Nation. It's a wonder none of them squirt-bomb the car. I guess they're too busy to think about purging, or evacuating, or any such mundane movements. I inch along tossing crackers. Graceful gulls follow, dancing on air like divas on display. A fleet of elegance follows me to the edge of the park where I empty what's left of the mini-crackers and watch the gulls touch down for the final time. It is one beautiful sight!

I wonder if they will know me when I return.

I wonder if they'll yell: *"Hey Lady, ya' got any food?"*

I'd better stop at Food-for-Less and pick up some more goodies for my new friends.

Ever see a trained sea-gull?

Ever train one yourself?

Well, believe it - or not!

GRAY DAYS

The postman is gray-haired, thick-skinned, and red like a lobster. He looks to be about seventy-five. He blows smoke-rings out the door as he moves his mail truck around the parking lot across from the emergency room. Although I never see him distribute any letters, I watch as he drives around the outbuildings on hospital grounds.

An elderly woman climbs into the battered, gray Chevy parked next to me. She cranks that old dinosaur up and lets it idle. It coughs up greenhouse gases while she speaks frantically to someone on the other end of her cell phone. I push buttons and roll up the windows in my van. 'Green-gas' is upset about 'grandma' who refuses to be admitted to the hospital, but needs a shot every twelve hours. The shots could be administered at home, the doctor said, but granny balked at the $200.00 per diem. And they need to draw more fluid off grandma's lungs, but granny is expecting family to visit from out-of-town so she insists on going home, even if she dies. Granny has decided to let 'Green-gas', her elderly granddaughter, drive her to Emergency every day for her shots and treatment. After all, she must be home for her guests! If this granddaughter won't do it, granny told the doctor, her other granddaughter will.

The loud voice of the agitated woman tells the other end of the line that she has had enough. She just can't take it anymore. "You handle it," she roars into the cell phone.

Her frustration flies out of her car window, slices its way through exhaust fumes, and circles the murky air until it finds its way back to her telephone. I turn on my air conditioning. It's getting stuffy in my car with the windows rolled up. The dog and I can't breathe.

'Green-gas' finally hangs up the phone. She slams her old hoopty of a car into reverse, rears out of the parking space in a cloud of choking black smoke, leaving me wondering where the heck she's going. *"Hey, Green-gas, where are you going? What's going to happen to granny? Hey! Granny is still inside!"*

Clouds roll across the skies and over the Red Oaks and Christmas Pines that line the parking lot. A gentle breeze keeps vigil over waiting vehicles. "Emergency Parking Only," so the sign reads. Behind the sign, a towering fern rustles against a red brick building where I now see a row of mailboxes hidden behind neatly trimmed hedges. Oh, that's where the postman delivered! His truck blocked the view of the mailboxes.

When the smoke dissipated and the smell was gone I turned off the air-conditioner and opened the car windows. I waited a while, but 'Green-gas' did not return.

He couldn't breathe. His chest hurt and he could barely move. That's why we brought him here. He's hooked up to a heart monitor and he's asleep. They haven't decided whether to keep him or let him go. I wait in the car and pray. His dog won't stop whining. I count the vegetation as I watch cars and people come and go. I sift snatches of conversation from the odd eyes that wander by.

The sun tries to peep through the haze but it's a gray day, filled with winners, losers, and the muted drone of prayer.

FIREWORKS

Don't say fireworks too loudly because not everyone is thinking celebration.

Some try to take shelter in silence – hearts beating louder than the sound of gunfire. Three, five, eight, nine shots. Three, five, eight, nine bodies. A South Carolina bible study.

Don't close your eyes and pretend you don't know what happened here. Even blind eyes see what's happened. Listen to the fireworks.

You've heard it before. You are hearing it again. Rapid fire. Gunfire. Fireworks.

Let the ricochet echo loudly in your brain so you will remember next time - and perhaps take action - if only to open your mouth in protest, and mean it.

Put your fireworks where they will do some good. Not on stage – for show – but in jurisprudence.

Three, five, eight, nine shots. Three, five, eight, nine bodies. Bible study in a South Carolina church.

There is too much talk. And with every deadly explosion some fool praises the fireworks.

TOO BLACK

He had burns on his body that his great-grandmother put there when he was born. He was too dark, she said, *"too black,"* and she threw him in the fire to spare him a life of misery and certain torture in a white world.

But the midwife snatched him from the fire, carried him away, hid him out, treated his wounds, kept him alive, protected him from danger, kept him and raised him as her own.

Mama Rosa had herself a son. She had family and so did he. Ricky grew to love her like no other, for he knew no other. No one ever came for him. No one ever looked for him.

His burns healed. A few scars remained to tell the story but he grew tall and thick, was quick to smile, and smart like Mama Rosa who paid his way through his college years by providing live chickens for his chow hall. He graduated with honors and a Doctorate.

Mama Rosa beamed as Rick led the short line of Talladega graduates, the slight limp in his left leg barely noticeable any more. Mama's hand-me-down therapies and old home remedies worked wonders.

As he accepted his diploma he turned and waved at Mama. Huge tears trickled down her proud cheeks. *"Ricco! Mio figlio!"* she cried, *"Lui è così bello"*. She translated to the other mother's. "My son!" she said, "He is so beautiful!"

THE LETTER

The gate creaked open and the old woman shuffled her way to the other side. She put all her weight on the walker and took several deep breaths, relaxing before she could begin again.

She was alone. She was ninety-nine years old, all alone, and today was her birthday.

The wide-brim hat hid her eyes from the blistering noon day sun. Lunch would have to wait today; there were far more important matters. Today there would be a letter.

She shaded her eyes as she surveyed the path to the mailbox. The red-clay trail glistened like patent-leather under the fertile sun. She took another step.

She dragged that right foot as she pushed and pulled the walker over the coarse ground. The road was rocky and uneven. Heavy rains always dug new potholes for her to find. She pulled her crooked body a few more inches before she had to stop and rest again.

The old farmhouse sat nestled in a clearing less than a mile from the main highway where the mailman made his rounds. Wooden planks covered recurring ravines that pelting rains had cut into her road. There was no one around to repair flood damage anymore. She did everything herself.

Today there would be a letter...

Flashbacks!

She took a deep breath, exhaling determination. She clutched the walker and dragged that troublesome right foot heavily across decaying boards. The first set of creaky planks gave her a hard time as they rocked and shifted under her weight. The walker was warm to her touch. She repositioned her hands and steadied herself. She wrapped one corner of her apron around the walkers' sun-blistered handles while she used the other end of the calico to wipe sweat from her brow.

She listened for a moment to her own shallow breathing.

Squirrels scurried up the trees where they could watch her.

She took no note of squirrels today. She had nothing for them. No nuts. No seeds. Nothing.

Instead, she pulled his old watch fob from her apron pocket and studied it while she labored and blessed the momentary shade under the towering pines. After a few more deep breaths she smiled and put the watch back in her pocket.

It was ten past two.

She was almost there.

Today, there would be a letter...

THE PLAGUE OF DR. LAMIA

They were in love and planning to be married before the big sickness changed him. That's why she worked so hard to become a doctor, so that she could find a cure, and cure especially, him. He was one of the first to fall prey to the disease.

When 60% of the retiring little village had succumbed to the contagion, the unaffected 40% began to pack up and leave, terrified of the dreaded Belugosi Syndrome, an epidemic whose origin was traced back to the bite of a tiny rabid bat.

Jean-Carl was among the first victims. At Stage Five of the illness, the love of her life was now, chromatically, a full- blown vampire. She had to save him.

As "Doctor" Christine Lamia she could use her medical credentials, the new blood bank she had created to treat infection by indirect method, and her hematology center to complete the necessary research. After all, her processes had kept her own infection at a Stage Two level, and the reversal procedure she developed looked extremely promising.

Time. Just a little more time. All she needed was a little more time and she could set Jean-Carl free. She could save him.

She looked longingly at her wedding dress hanging crisply over the bathroom door. She entertained quick visions of their wedding day as she raced to lock the windows and strap the heavy wooden barricades into place. It would be dark soon and this was the first night of the maiden moon. There was much to be done.

The clinic reeked of freshly cut garlic. Dozens of strategically placed mirrors were draped in raw clove pods. Echinacea leaves boiled in aluminum steam-pots. The combination of scents was found to be toxic to the undead.

The Doctor settled in for the long lunar vigil. She bathed her body in crushed Hawthorne Berries and ingested Chaparral herbs to protect against vampiric cell growth. She prepared and drank profusely of a haemostatic tincture of Horsetail and Yellow Paint Root, which would cleanse and protect her liver and purify her blood in case the barricades were breached. She increased her intake of Bilberry tea to lower her blood sugar. Low blood sugar is imperative in the prevention of Belugosi Syndrome. She had instructed the villagers what to do. They all had Dr. Lamia's Mandrake Spritzer guns. A moderate dose to the face of the carrier would serve as paralytic, instantly lowering ph levels while Lamia Serum penetrated skin cells, purifying blood toxins on contact. Only Lamia understood this chemistry.

The villagers didn't care about chemistry; they just wanted to end the plague. Lamia had the entire village armed and alert. They knew what they had to do and they were ready. Now they waited and prayed for a short night and quick daybreak.

Lamia cornered Jean-Carl.

DARK WATERS

The bubbles burst the surface of the dark water with barely a sound. Only the fish knew there was something amiss. When the sun came up there was not a trace of Goldie. They looked everywhere for her, her friends did, but she was nowhere to be found. Her car was still right where she had parked it. The keys were in the ignition but Goldie was gone. Each one of the partiers was quizzed by the Boston Police Department although the department didn't really care. Goldie was an outsider and not important to their community. "You don't have to look too hard," the detective told the beat cops. "Don't waste a lot of time on this one. Just go through the motions for the locals and make a statement to the media about drugs, or gang related activity or something like that and we can put this thing to bed. Get it over with. I've got things to do and I'm sure you do too!"

The beat cops asked a few questions of the party guests, took a few notes on slim, yellow notepads, and let everybody go.

The next day the headlines and the six o'clock news briefly mentioned the *suicide* of Goldie Parks, Civil Rights Activist and leader of the Regiment for Rights Party of the eastern United States.

"Goldie was 6'6", 280 pounds," the broadcaster announced. "He is survived by his wife, Leslie, and six children," he continued. "While campaigning for a seat on the Defense League of America, Goldie apparently fell victim to complications of a personal nature, faltered, and took his own life. Burial details for Mr. Parks are currently unknown."

Well at least they got her name right.

Goldie Parks.

Her name is Goldie Parks.

FOREVER

The pain was so severe that she couldn't raise her head. She screamed each time she tried, so she quickly gave up and lay on the sofa in a pool of tears, sweat rising from her body like steam.

He freaked out! Didn't know what to do! He didn't want to touch her because he didn't know how not to hurt her.

What a night! It was supposed to be a quiet evening between the two of them. They were celebrating an anniversary of sorts. It was the second year since they had made a commitment to each other. They had big plans for their lives and were in no big rush because they had made "forever" their promise.

They danced and popped champagne all afternoon. It was well into evening when the food was delivered. They arranged the table and lit dinner candles which had burned halfway down when she keeled over and couldn't move. Pain took her swiftly. It took control of her body and finally consumed her while he twisted in panic. At least he had presence of mind enough to answer the phone when it rang. It was Aunt Margie calling from Chicago to wish them "Happy Forever".

Margie managed to get some sort of story out of David before she got hold of Cicely who lived just five minutes from the hotel where David and Susan were staying. "Sissy" contacted emergency services and was still on the phone with dispatch when she made it to the hotel, just minutes after she got Aunt Margie's phone call. When she got to the room, David (her first cousin on her fathers' side) was sprawled across the floor clutching the cold blue hand that dangled from the couch.

Paramedics were on the way. Cicely stayed on the line with a 911 dispatcher who rapid-fired questions at her, trying to ascertain the problem so he could offer the right type of assistance. His blind assessment of the situation wasn't doing anybody any good.

Sirens faded and stopped. Sissy opened the door and left it standing open for the paramedics. In moments, a crew of five came through the door and pushed David out of the way. Sissy hung up the phone.

"Forever," David mumbled. "Forever!"

Paramedics prepped the patient for transport. With the last needle in place, pulse checked, oxygen strapped to her chin, and prayer offered up for a little color to break through her ashen pallor, a comatose Susan was wheeled down a hallway, past curious on-lookers, and raced to County General.

David was still sprawled out on the floor mumbling 'forever' when they wheeled his woman away.

SELAH

He designed his own casket. In it were pictures he selected from mountains and mountains of reflections of himself. He wanted to be sure he kept good company on his way to the after-life, so he covered the silver-satin lining of his bronze casket with his best pictures. He was drop dead gorgeous. A good looking man. He said so himself - many times.

Planning his own funeral started off as a sad endeavor because a person of his caliber should be excluded from death and demise. He should live forever. That's the way he saw it and planned it, but Mother Nature didn't agree. She considered him just another ordinary mortal despite all his arguments to the contrary.

In time, however, he took pleasure in the planning. He lined his casket with his favorite cameos. Shots that he could (and would) enjoy on his journey to the next realm where he'd shine and sparkle like a person of his significance should shine and sparkle! He couldn't help that. After all, he was a wonderful man. He said so himself - often.

He picked the scent he would wear on his journey. It was heady and sweet. Cheap! A broke woman's scent in an oil base that left a sickening trail in his wake as he strutted and switched his way down his private aisles! "They love me," he smirked to himself. "I know they're watching me, I can feel their eyes." He left them choking on the scent of him while he misinterpreted the reason. "See how they praise me," he assured himself as they fanned their noses and held their breath. He ignored them. Actually took their waving as an insult! "How dare they attempt to speak to me. Unsolicited communication! The nerve of them! They must not know who I am!"

He dressed the part. The part of his own magnificence. The suit was dark. The shirt was pink. The tie matched the shirt in color and flare. Belt and shoes were crisp, unyielding, and made him swagger. He swaggered until his hips rolled. He moved like a woman; smacking of femininity. There were whispers!

He prepared the guest list. A register of important people who were to be invited to his final festivities. He assigned each guest a number according to the level of their importance.

He selected his speakers and presented them with copies of the words they were to deliver at his eulogy. He was meticulous in his final arrangements. Scrupulous in this final tribute to himself. He orchestrated what was to be said and how he was to be praised. He selected the music, the organist, and the soloists. Nothing was left to chance. Everything had to be just so! Everything would be perfect! This was his final show you know. His penultimate final finale. (Drat mother nature!)

He designed the seating chart and used his numbers system to fill in the blanks. Bodies would be placed just so. The most important would have closest proximity to his casket. They deserved the best, first-hand, last look at him. For the ones seated farther back, a life-sized portrait would be centered and projected on the walls surrounding the altar. He posed especially for this shot in preparation for the event. He was beautiful. Drop dead gorgeous! He said so himself - repeatedly.

He made sure he selected the projector and projectionist for this final tribute. He drew up a contract and had it signed.

There were alternative clauses included should there be any change in circumstances. Anything unforeseen, like rain, fog, or any overcast affecting his lighting. He left no stone unturned. After all, he was a brilliant man. He said so himself - constantly.

Plans finalized, he took his seat at his work station, his back to his clientele, his eyes gazing at the latest photo secured in the non-glare glass frame at the front edge of his desk. The photo stared back at him as he stared at himself. "What a good looking fellow," he told himself - incessantly.

Selah!

GREAT IS THE GLORY

Gregory preached a hellfire sermon! He talked about God as if he knew Him personally, and since he had personal knowledge of the Maker of Us All, that meant that the rest of the world didn't, and his congregation (the ones who latched onto and followed every breath Gregory took) had to wait for Gregory to interpret and relay all direct messages from God.

But Theodora was not such a good follower. She was one of those "feminists" who believed she could think for herself and she demanded the freedom to do just that. She told the minister on many an irate occasion that she needed no middle-man in her pursuit of The Almighty. Glory to God, she could (and would) talk to God by herself and for herself.

Pastor Gregory did not like Theodora. He put up with her because her father was one of the wealthiest deacons in the church. Pastor didn't dare antagonize Deacon Thrasher.

And so it went.

Theodora stood out like swollen ankles, forcing Gregory to concoct ways, plans, and plots to get rid of Theodora Thrasher. To get her out of his parish.

But Theodora was no dummy. She claimed a personal relationship with her God and she prayed incessantly on the subject of Pastor Michael Gregory.

On January 28, during a fitful, rip-roaring sermon about

false prophets, Pastor Gregory slipped and fell from the pulpit. His leg broke in three places. Healing would take approximately one year the doctors said. Then there would be rehab.

Meanwhile, the congregation was without, and calling for a leader. And since the most outstanding voice in their community came from Deacon Thrashers' fiery daughter, Theodora *(who was willing to lead),* Theodora became interim director of Great is the Glory Non-denominational House of Paradise Worship Center.

Deacon Thrasher was pleased. Theodora was in her glory. And Pastor Gregory? Well, Pastor Gregory applied for transfer to a different locale. He had always wanted a cooler climate anyway, and as soon as he could control the fancy walking sticks attached above his elbows he would be on his way.

"Never trust a feminist!" Rehab personnel heard the pastor repeatedly ranting this phrase. "Never trust a feminist!" "Never trust a feminist!" Pastor informed one of the concerned orderlies that he was preparing his next sermon.

From the tiny bits and pieces that the orderly overheard, he determined that *whenever* Pastor Gregory got to *wherever* Pastor Gregory was going, Pastor Gregory was going to preach one hellfire sermon!!

... and all the people said:
"amen"

Dolly A. Dixon

Jeannette DesBoine

EIGHT

ME AND MRS. MASON
(diary & journal of a teenaged girl)

Hi! I'm Michelle Nelson. I'm sixteen going on seventeen. I was eleven when I came to live at my cousin Debra's house. She was almost thirteen but we were just about the same size. We could wear each other's clothes, but Uncle Jeff and Aunt Maggie got mad when we did. Once I heard Aunt Maggie whisper to Debra that I was not to wear any of her things, or else! But Debra and I were friends. I really liked her and she treated me like a sister. We told everybody at school that we were "sister-cousins" and we laughed when they didn't understand what we meant.

There are only two bedrooms in the house so I shared Debra's room. We told each other our deepest secrets and dreams, and we giggled long into the night, way after it was "lights out time" in our room.

I did odd jobs around the neighborhood to earn my keep. Mama would have wanted it that way. I bought my own school clothes and shoes with the money I earned cleaning old Mrs. Mason's kitchen. I didn't have much, but what I had was mine.

Mrs. Mason still lives in the big brown house next door. The porch is covered in honeysuckle vines with pink and white blossoms that smell like the sweet perfume mama used to wear when she got all dressed up to go out somewhere special. I love that smell.

I thought Mrs. Mason was pretty old when I met her. I didn't ask her, but she was at least forty-five or fifty. She was older than Uncle Jeff and Aunt Maggie, but boy could she cook! It always smelled good at her house, and she didn't mind feeding me as long as I cleaned the kitchen her way. That meant I had to keep everything spotless. That's what she called it: spotless. I even had to keep the pots shining. She taught me how to use steel wool to scrape the pots clean (and my fingertips raw). The stove and the floors had to be kept spotless too. She used a couple of wire brushes to get those jobs done, a little one with a fine mesh for the stove, and a wide, flat one with bristles as stiff as a board for the floor. She let me use her floppy rubber gloves to protect my knuckles. The red gloves were for the stove. The crackly yellow ones for the floor. Even the gloves had to be thoroughly washed each time they were used. And afterward, wiped dry and hung on their very own rack in the broom closet. Mrs. Mason was real picky and particular about her kitchen, but we got to be really good friends. She was like my own grandmother. Like my mother too. She was like the two people I missed the most in life. I didn't mind working for her. She liked how I did my job and she liked talking to me about school and life and whatever I wanted to talk about. She told me stories about her life. About the way things used to be and the way things ought to be. She said I was a good listener, and I do love listening to her. I love the way she laughs. When she smiles her eyes sparkle and kind of twitch like they're dancing.

The second summer I was in Pine Bluff, Mrs. Mason and I went into business together. We really did! I was so excited about it that I couldn't wait to get started. We talked about it a long time. We talked about cooking and selling something from her kitchen! Everything she made was good. I get hungry just thinking about it. She showed me how to cook a few easy dishes. I liked baking cookies best of all, so when we talked about what we would sell, I suggested cookies of course. She said okay but told me I would have to learn something about business before we got started. She had me write down all the questions and ideas I could come up with. Then, when I finished my list, she said we would talk business and make a plan. That plan was about six weeks in the making. I never worked harder at anything in my life. It was hard, but it was fun learning so much stuff. I wrote out what Mrs. Mason called the *business plan*. Questions kept coming up as she explained more and more things to me, so I added new questions and ideas to my list. "We are about to enter into a *joint venture*," Mrs. Mason announced to me one morning. I had no idea what a joint venture was until she smiled and said it simply meant that we were *partners*, in business together. I thought I would die I was so proud. "We are *entrepreneurs*," she added. Then she made me look up the word entrepreneur in the dictionary and read the definition to her. I had to study the definition until I had it memorized, then we would start our business. It was an easy word to remember, and when I repeated the definition to her with no hesitation, our business venture started.

The plan we put on paper (or *"drafted"* to quote Mrs. Mason) was that she would bake tons of sugar cookies and I would wrap, package and sell them at school, at church, and around the neighborhood. We would split the money 50/50 after *costs*. *Costs* was another business term I had to learn. We had to pay for the ingredients to make the cookies and we had to wrap the cookies in something so we could sell them. We couldn't just hand out unwrapped cookies! That's nasty. Germs! Yuk! We had to buy ingredients and packaging materials in order to make and sell our *product*.

The costs of the ingredients: butter; flour; sugar; eggs; vanilla; cream, and the costs of the packaging supplies: waxed paper; tin foil; brown paper bags, would come out first. That was our investment or *"seed"* money, she explained. Those were our costs. The costs of goods sold, or *cogs* said in still another way. Ms. Mason is so smart. I kept a little spiral notebook so I could write down everything she said. Everything I learned I shared with

Debra. I hoped that Debra would join us, but Aunt Maggie had other plans for Debbie.

Anyway, once Mrs. Mason was satisfied that I knew the definition of entrepreneur and that I understood the basic beginnings of our business, we went grocery shopping. When we got everything we needed we brought it home and put it away. Then we sat at the kitchen table while Mrs. Mason had me add up all the receipts for what we had bought to make and package our cookies. I did the math. I kept the books, Mrs. Mason said! She made me the *bookkeeper*. Imagine that! Me! The bookkeeper! Mrs. Mason said she would help me and show me how. Mrs. Mason can help you do and learn anything. I started calling her Grammy Mason. Sometimes Grams. She called me "Misha." Short for Michelle. That's what Mama used to call me; Misha.

On our first batch of cookies Grams and I spent $3.00 on 10 pounds of flour; $3.00 on 20 pounds of sugar; $1.50 for a dozen eggs; $1.00 for vanilla flavoring; $1.00 for butter; and $1.00 for cream. The total cost of the ingredients added up to $10.50. That was our *sub-total*. According to Grams, it was our *sub*-total because that wasn't all. We also had to add on the cost of the packaging supplies we bought. All the receipts added together would give us what she called the *grand-total*. Everything combined.

We spent $1.00 for aluminum foil *(Grammy Mason calls it tin-foil)*; $1.00 for waxed paper; and $1.50 for lunch bags. That total was $3.50. Adding the two totals together (the cost of the ingredients plus the cost of the wrap and packaging stuff) our cost of goods sold came to a grand total of $14.00. I liked being the bookkeeper. Math is really easy when Grams explains it. She handed me a large brown envelope. "Write COSTS on the top right hand corner," she said. "Put the month and date on the top left corner and write our $14.00 grand total bottom center. We're going to have to add the price of these *manila* envelopes to our cogs. We'll buy a pack next time we shop. That's a bookkeeping expense. We need it to do business" That made sense. I did what Grams said and put the envelope on the kitchen counter so I would know where it was. Grams called that envelope a *cost sheet.* All the receipts for the month would be filed in their own monthly envelopes. "That will keep bookkeeping simple," Grams said. "Especially when we start doing taxes," she added.

I hope I explained that right, diary! Grams can explain it better, but meanwhile, I needed another explanation about costs of goods sold because we hadn't sold anything yet and I didn't quite get it. 'How can we have costs of goods sold when we haven't sold anything? We haven't even *made* the cookies yet,' I whined at Grams. "No matter," Grams said. "Just think of it as the cost of the things we *have to* buy in order to make the things we are *going* to sell. It takes money to make money; you've heard that saying haven't you?" "Well, yes I have heard that saying," I told her. "Then think about the future," she said. "In this case, it's the cost of the goods that *will be* sold." She wrote 2B on my notebook then said "2B or not 2B. Already sold or *to be* sold, you have to pay for the stuff to make your product don't you? Remember when we talked about seed money? Well, think of it as more seeds. I'll explain later."

Grams wanted to know where I wanted to keep our business money. She said it needed to be kept separate from other money and suggested that I find something to use for a bank. I looked around in the kitchen and found an empty cookie jar on the shelf in the pantry. She told me that her son had given her that jar on one of her long ago birthdays. She agreed to let me use it if I promised to be very careful and not chip it or break it. I promised to take extra good care of her special jar which was shaped like a puffed up green toad frog. Mrs. Mason collected frogs. She had ceramic frogs all over the house. Her husband and son had given them to her over the years. She had a special place and name for each of them. This one was called "Ernie," after her son who drowned in a boating accident when he was little. Cookie jar Ernie had been resting safely on a shelf in the back of the pantry ever since the real Ernie's accident. "It was a long time ago." Mrs. Mason stared at the jar for a minute then told me to bring the receipts for the $14.00. We put the receipts in the cost sheet envelope, stuck the envelope inside Ernie, put his head back on, and put him back in the pantry. "We just accounted for our investment money," Mrs. Mason said. That was Sunday afternoon. Grams decided we would start on our product the next Friday, after school. That seemed like such a long time to me. I had a really hard time waiting. I was ready to start baking cookies right then. Right that minute. Right that very second!

Friday finally came. Grammy Mason baked twenty-four dozen cookies. She made each one the size of a pie plate! She baked cookies all day Friday and all day Saturday. I could only help after school on Friday, but I helped almost all day on Saturday, as soon as I finished my chores for Aunt Maggie and Uncle Jeff. Part of my job was to figure out how many cookies were in twenty-four dozen so I could bag them up properly. Of course I know that a dozen is twelve of anything, but I had to know exactly how many cookies we were talking about in order to figure how many bags were needed. I figured that Mrs. Mason had baked 288 cookies because one dozen is 12 and she made 24 dozen and 24 times 12 is 288. We were going to package the big sugar cookies in sets of three and sell each set for a dollar, so, if I was going to put three cookies in each bag I would divide 288 cookies by 3. Three into 288 goes 96 times. I needed 96 bags. One hundred bags come in the package we purchased at the grocery store. Just right! With a few left over!

Grams and I wrapped and packaged 96 bags of cookies. We folded sets of three cookies in sheets of wax paper then sealed the sheets in aluminum foil. The wax paper might unfold, but the foil wouldn't. The cookies couldn't come loose and crumble with the foil sealing them together. Each bag was to be sold for one dollar. *(2B. I thought about my lesson on cogs.)* Sunday I sold cookies after church and gave the money to Mrs. Mason for safe-keeping. Monday I took cookies to school in a wagon and sold them to my teachers, my friends, to the janitor and to the cooks in the kitchen. Everybody bought some. On my way home I sold cookies house to house and door to door. Before I got home that Monday I had sold all ninety-six bags. Some people bought three and four bags! My heart was bursting with pride. I had money stuffed in my lunch box and was pulling the empty wagon and running so fast to get home to show Mrs. Mason that I tripped on the porch steps and fell through the screen door. Mrs. Mason helped me up. She was laughing so hard when she dusted me off that she didn't seem to notice or mind that I had destroyed her door. "That's okay little one," she told me. "We'll fix that later."

Mrs. Mason said I was quite the salesperson. She poured a big glass of tea and sat me down at the table to catch my breath. She put a straw in the tea and turned on the fan to cool me off. I was anxious to get to my bookkeeping so I pulled out my record book from the kitchen drawer and started figuring.

Including the money I had given her on Sunday, we had made a total of $96.00. $48.00 for me and $48.00 for her. 50/50. Wow! I liked being an entrepreneur!

I heard Mrs. Mason talking to me about *net-profit* and cogs. Oh, rats! I had forgotten about the cogs. I ran to the pantry to get Ernie. I took out the *cost sheet* envelope and the receipts for the $14.00 that was our seed money. Our investment capital! How could I forget the fourteen-dollars that it cost us to make and sell our product? Now I had to re-figure our profit. We sold 96 bags and made a *total* of $96.00 {that was our *gross* Mrs. Mason noted} but we had to subtract the $14.00 start-up costs. Even so, I could tell by the pile of money on the table that we had done good business. I did the math while Mrs. Mason took fourteen crisp one-dollar bills from the pile and stuffed them down Ernie's neck. She screwed his head back on and put him back in the pantry for our next adventure. I checked my bookkeeping against the cash on the table. It came out the same. "Did you *balance*," Mrs. Mason asked me. I knew immediately what her question meant. "Yes, Grams, we balanced." The figures and the cash were equal. I shot Grams a smile so wide I started drooling. We both cracked up laughing as I wiped my soggy lips and chin on the back of my hand.

Back to my notebook. After the fourteen dollars was paid back, Mrs. Mason labeled the rest of our money *net-profit*. The *gross* or *total* amount of money we made from the sale minus the *cogs* was the net-profit. Guess how much we made! Even after we took out Ernie's $14.00 from the $96.00, we had a net-profit of $82.00. That was my lesson for the day.

I re-checked the figures on the books. Then I counted the cash again and placed it in two equal stacks. Grammy's and mine. 50/50. I couldn't stop smiling and Grams was tickled by my excitement. I was happy! Forty-one dollars for me and forty-one dollars for her. *Net. Net.*

I asked Grams what she was going to do with her share of the profits and she told me she was going to save it for something special. I decided to save mine for something special too. I let Grams put my money in her bank account until I get enough cash to open a savings account of my own. You need $100.00 to open an account at Grammy's bank.

"I'll have that real soon," I told Grammy. "Real soon."

My next business lesson would be about taxes, Grams told me. This first time we weren't going to worry about it. "It'll be our little secret this time," she said. "We won't tell the tax-man because he didn't do any of the work so he doesn't deserve any of the profit." The next word I had to look up was e-x-e-m-p-t (exempt). I ran to get the big dictionary.

Grammy Mason is so much fun. I love her. I love her as much as I love her sugar cookies and enjoy hearing her tease me about eating up all the profits. We've been in business four years now. She still puts a few cookies aside for both of us to eat at tea-time and on business meeting day, which is every Friday after school. We eat sugar cookies and drink tea brewed in an old fashioned coffee pot with the insides removed. It's just like making coffee but we use tea bags instead of coffee grounds. And we talk. We talk about business. We laugh and joke around about school. And, if I need any help, she helps me with my homework. She even listens to me talk about cute boys at school and then she warns me about growing up too fast. But that's another story.

Life at cousin Debra's house is different. Nobody smiles much. Debra is still like a big sister to me, just like the day we met. We giggle in secret and plan fun stuff to do when we're outside the house. She doesn't work like I do, but she has other activities that take up her time. Church and school! School and church! Debra's folks plan for Debra to be a doctor one day. Or at least a nurse. They insist on it. And Debra *wants* to be a doctor, so she's always studying. She has to get excellent grades, and she does.

I make excellent grades too because Mrs. Mason says I'll need good grades to be successful in business and she helps me study to make sure I stay at the top of my class, grade wise. I spend so much time with Mrs. Mason that people think we're kin. But my real kin are Debra, Uncle Jeff and Aunt Maggie. Uncle Jeff is my dad's brother. Jefferson Jerome Nelson is his full name.

Some of his really old friends from when he was a kid still call him Jay-Jay. He hates that!

I lost dad in Viet Nam. I don't want to remember or talk about that right now. Mama died the following year and that's when Aunt Maggie and Uncle Jeff took me in. Uncle Jeff looks just like daddy except for his mouth. Daddy had a smiley mouth. Uncle Jeff has a mouth like a doctor. Like Debra's mouth until I make her laugh!

I have one other living relative. At least I have no reason to believe that Grandpa Nelson is not still alive. His name is Richard Nelson and he's Uncle Jeff's and daddy's father. Before daddy shipped out he located grandpa in a homeless shelter. Everybody there called him "Big Richard." When they found him, Mama and daddy took me to see him. I haven't forgotten. I remember he had the darkest eyes I've ever seen. Eyes that look right through you. He looked really old and really small for a man as tall as he was when he stood up. Daddy said he was 6'6". When we visited with him we found him huddled in a corner chair staring out the window of this tiny little room. He had an old dingy trench coat draped over his knees. The coat was grimy with street dirt. It was a short visit and when we were done Daddy gave him a card from his friend who was a legal advisor, and a piece of paper with our address and phone number on it. Daddy was shipping out at four in the morning. Grandpa said he would call mama the next day to arrange to go home with her and live with us. He never called, and when mama and I came back to check on him, he was gone. Nobody knew where he went. We tried to find him, but we couldn't. After mama got sick she never saw him again. I saw him though. Even though nobody believes me, I saw him.

I saw an old man in a dirty old trench coat standing in the field just outside the chain-link fence at the cemetery when daddy was buried. He was almost as tall as the fence. I was in the hearse when I saw him watching. I could see his eyes. The darkest eyes I have ever seen. They were like deep sink holes in a black road and they were wet with tears that left long streaks down his rusty cheeks. The instant I saw him I knew it was grandpa. I glanced out the back window and saw the grungy old coat bend in half and plop down on the damp ground. I tried to get mama to turn the car around but she insisted that it was not Grandpa Nelson and that was the end of it. I was ten years old. The next year mama was buried next to daddy and I came to live at Debra's house. I've been here going on six years now, but I remember it like it was yesterday.

"Big Richard" is alive. I know he's alive. Nobody at Debra's house ever talks about him, but I know he's still alive. When I try to bring up the subject they just cut me off. They say I don't know what I'm talking about. They won't listen and they won't let me talk about it. I know what I'm saying, though. I know what I saw.

***

Dear Diary: It's been so long since we've talked, you've turned into a journal. We haven't spoken since Mrs. Mason took sick. Well, to bring you up to date, even when Mrs. Mason got sick she still took time with me, and I took care of her as much as I could. I was fifteen when I started working at her house every day. She paid me what she could and she taught me to cook like she cooked. She sat at the kitchen table and told me what to do. "Write this down now baby, so you won't forget, in case I don't feel too good." That's what she said and that's what I did. My new notebook filled with recipes and instructions. Aunt Maggie and Uncle Jeff didn't mind my staying with Grammy Mason so I spent a lot of time with her. When she got really bad off and had a hard time getting up and walking around they let me move in with her. As long as I stayed in school and kept my grades up I'd be allowed to live there. And since Aunt Maggie and Uncle Jeff were right next-door, they would help out whenever Mrs. Mason and I needed anything. Uncle Jeff made sure she got to the doctor's office. Aunt Maggie took care of any errands she might need. I shopped, did the banking, cooked and cleaned, and Debra came every day to do the nursing parts. She bathed Mrs. Mason and put her to bed and combed her hair and things like that. They get along really well. Mrs. Mason has so much love to give to everybody. Debra smiled a lot more and laughed out loud at Mrs. Mason's jokes. I could tell she liked spending time with us, and I love having her around.

But Debra Lynne went and got herself pregnant before she finished school. Aunt Maggie almost had a stroke when she found out. She told Debra to get out of her house and stay out. She couldn't live at home anymore. Uncle Jeff tried to have a family meeting for them to discuss it and make plans but the timing just wasn't right. Aunt Maggie started throwing things at Debra and Debra darted out the back door and was in Mrs. Mason's kitchen before we knew it. Mrs. Mason was sitting at the table listening to all the commotion. I guess the whole neighborhood heard it.

Debra flopped down in the chair next to Mrs. Mason, put her head on the table and began to cry. I took Debra Lynne to my room so she could lie down on my bed. We talked about things. About Aunt Maggie for one thing. About planning for another. What was she going to do with her life? About school? About the baby and all? First off, Debra needed a place to stay.

Mrs. Mason heard us talking and said we could both stay at her house. Grams has a big house and an even bigger heart. I was already there and Debra moved in right away. We went to her house to get her things while Aunt Maggie was at church on Sunday morning. It was one week before Thanksgiving. We prayed that we would always have plenty to be thankful for. Debra Lynne took care of Mrs. Mason and I took care of the house and the cooking. That's how it was. We were all thankful to have each other. Mrs. Mason had her social services worker hire Debra as her care-giver. She helped Debra use the money she earned to finish high school. She also taught Debra how to save her money so she could pay for nursing school after the birth of the baby. Debra will start with an LVN license. Licensed Vocational Nurse. Mrs. Mason said that once Debra gets that LVN license she can take it from there to anywhere she wants to go. Debra and her little fat belly got busy!

Mrs. Mason seemed to get better and better with the care and activity around the house. And when little Jimmy Lee was finally born she took to him like he was her own. She decided she would take him in and make it her business to watch him while Debra continued school. Mrs. Mason and little Jimmy Lee are next door right now, visiting with Aunt Maggie and Uncle Jeff. They want Debra to come back home. She's thinking about it but she doesn't want to leave her care-giver job or Mrs. Mason.

Well, diary, I've got cookies to bake. The cookie business is booming! And it won't run itself. I've got work to do.

P.S. You know, diary, one of these days I'm going to have a little girl and I'm going to name her Marguerite. Michelle Marguerite or Marguerite Michelle, named after me and Mrs. Mason. I'll call her "Misha" like me. She's gonna be smart and loving and kind and strong just like Grammy Mason. She and I will go into business together; a joint-venture called "Misha and Misha - Cookies for Cookie Lovers." I love that name. It sounds like money. Mrs. Mason says I might just want to get married first. Mrs. Mason is so funny.

Thank you for listening diary. I hope you got all that. I'll talk to you later. I've got lots of stuff to do...

BRIGHT AND BEAUTIFUL

Her eyes are open but they appear closed. They appear swollen shut because of deep wrinkles that cut into her flesh like craters across the surface of the moon. It's a beautiful face. A powerful face imprinted like a Mojave map. A face with many stories to tell.

Santa Fe suns created those craters in her skin. Severe heat and no shade aided the process. She was barely in her twenties when she first noticed lines in her cheeks. Each desert summer deepened the lines and every new year changed her appearance so swiftly that she finally didn't recognize the weather-beaten face in her own mirror.

When icy winter moons got in on the game they froze the craters created by summer sun into trenches solidified by ice and snow. And now, in addition to the hot wind, frigid northern airstreams of longevity add depths of character to her soul. Character lines! That's how they are called.

Another birthday approaches. She dreads the thought but reconciles vanity against reality and decides to give thanks for the ability to breathe in and out – life's basic music.

Things to Do Today! Somebody once gave her a birthday card with instructions for the day. She taped the card to her morning mirror and she starts every day by reading the card out loud. *Things to do today: Inhale, Exhale, Repeat!* That card gives her joy. It amuses her, makes her laugh, and causes her to look past the battered face in the looking-glass; past the old crone who has made her presence known in no uncertain terms; past the look of her to the soul of her - for in the soul of her rests a totally different entity! It's not the face anymore, it's the wisdom buried in each deep line and crevice that amazes her. It's the fact that life has taught her many things, has given her many experiences, and in running its course so far, has made her wise beyond encroaching years.

Pleasure and pain have rewards and consequences. Some consider pain a master teacher, but she disagrees. "Pain may be considered a most prolific teacher", she says, "but pleasure is the ultimate professor. Pain may lay the linoleum of understanding," she continues, "but pleasure furnishes each room. "

'So what do you see when you look at yourself in the mirror?' I ask her. She gazes at the glass, contemplating my question. I study her beauty and hear her soft reply: "I see music."

How does a person see music? I muse. Obviously, my confusion escapes me. I didn't intend to interrupt her but I had to dump the question and the anticipation from my mind. I had to say it out loud so I asked the actual question: 'How do you *see* music?'

She smiled and began again. "I see the music! I see the notes! The actual notes! I see them dancing in the air like your grandfather and I used to dance, almost airborne, floating in the atmosphere balanced on love. That was when we first discovered each other. We were merely children. Young. Raw. Uninhibited!"

"And then there are the dark notes of loss. Like when I lost my parents before I was old enough to imagine being without them. To this day the voices of my mother and father ride the dark notes."

"Then there are the sharps and the flats of birth, miscarriage, and loss of a child. Those notes float on memory cells and form the face of time eternal."

"And I see the music of success as clouds become mine to control. My hair has curled, straightened, and now thins. Mine eyes have traveled many miles from glint to haze."

"My music is here right now. It is painting pictures with the brush strokes of eternity. It can paint in any shade and on any shell. Music paints from the inside out. It paints from beginning to end. It paints my dancing heart in a swirling skirt, and my decaying years on a shell of solitude."

"And when the music passes the pallet to me I will use it to paint just what I see: the warmth and safety of my mother's womb and the beauty of life to be."

"All things bright and beautiful, the Lord God makes them all."

Flashbacks!

* * *

AFTERWORD

In answer to your question, stories are everywhere! There are stories in the mirror. There are stories in the sand. There are stories in fixed stares that haunt and devour the land. There are stories in that stack of papers overflowing the workroom chair; papers waiting to be sorted and filed; waiting to be acted upon while yellowing to the ash of age. Meanwhile, a sister-pile grows in an adjacent room; silently challenging the first pile; discretely replacing her, becoming her, perhaps even violently mocking her as sisters sometimes do.

There are stories in ragged assortments of coffee mugs; mugs telling unmatched tales about coffees and teas, and bourbons and cokes, and wet mornings when the sun won't shine and the blues drifts in through half-open windows and totally-closed hearts.

There are stories in circular patterns of dust. Dust on potted plants. Dust on leaves. Dust keeping vigil on the flow of oxygen. Dusty leaves whispering to each other in their own private language. Dusty leaves with roots cramped in pots too small to nurture growth. Dusty leaves stagnating in weak, worn-out soil. Dust laden leaves dropping like pennies with no fountain.

There are stories archived on pages of scrapbooks; pages recalling the past by trapping sketchy memories under plastic sheeting.

There are stories framed and hanging on sheet rocked walls; the frames accenting keepsakes too large to be sealed in scrapbooks; keepsakes reflecting a world long ago and far away.

There are stories in no longer used overnight cases filled with debilitating cosmetics; creams and potions in ornate jars where only a few precious drops remain, unused and unusable; their colors distorted, age-darkened, and hardened into wisdom. That ancient Samsonite™ locks around familiarity and buries it like precious treasure beneath the bathroom sink. New foundations accumulate, but never do they rival the perfections of the past.

There are stories in old newspaper clippings, cut and trimmed, pale and fading, edges curled, words no longer bold or bright; a barely legible record of what used-to-be, disintegrating in time.

There are stories in the clothes collecting in walk-in closets; clothes on special hangers; clothes awaiting proper moments in time and circumference; clothes piled tightly into one another, jammed and wedged into the creases of their neighbor.

There are stories in books beside the bed; books waiting to be read; unfinished chapters, dog-eared pages, bright covers beckoning a clock that keeps ticking and pointing its withering hands at forgotten promise.

There are stories in the ashes that line a glass bowl; ashes in an ashtray; ashes in an urn; ashes mixed with teardrops. *(Did you know that moistened ashes polish silver better than Brasso?)*

There are stories in the rain-stains on a ceiling.

There are stories in the whistle of a train.

FOOTNOTE

Flash!

In the course of writing, journaling, essaying, etc., children's stories made their way onto the scene. What a perfect time to break for them...

"The Homeless Cat" is based on a true incident. Yes, the cat was real (stuffed but real) and so is our main character, Shawn. And I'm sure you recognize the narrator.

While taking a breather from civic issues, the messages in "Me and Mrs. Mason" demanded to be addressed. As for the grammar of the title, set rules aside and break free! We're not doing rules today. Rules contain! The title is "Me and Mrs. Mason" for the sheer joy of it.

This entertaining collection of children's stories came about during transition from poetry to short story and reached out as teaching tools expressing ideals of tolerance as well as a few basic business precepts as presented in the 'Mason' diaries.

Stuff happens! And when it does, let it. It feeds need-to-know and nourishes need-to-be.

HUGS!

Flashbacks!

PUBLICATIONS

CHAPBOOKS

Through a Glass Door
Rumors of War
Trumpets, Flutes, and Alto Voices
Inner Visions
Eye to Eye
Port Costa People
The Bluest Blues
Home is Where Love Lives
What's Love Got to Do With It?
The Dead Man's Tongue
The Katrina Files
White Bread and Chocolate Milk
The Other Cheek
Rivers
Bitching

PLAYS

Motherland (Series 1, 2, 3)
Nina - Side 2

BOOKS

STORM! *(A Freewrite Diary and Workbook)*
DISASTER REVISITED! *(history/hot topics/cold files)*

ANTHOLOGIES

El Paso Community College Senior Adult Program

DOWN SENIOR STREET

A THOUSAND FRIDAYS

ABOUT THE AUTHOR

Jeannette DesBoine admits to being "possessed by the love of words and haunted by the spirit of the printed page." The University of Texas @ El Paso graduate describes herself as an English teacher by education, a writer by definition, and a poet with a passion for theater and spoken word.

Her journey into the art of writing began as newspaper reporter (Peninsula Bulletin, Palo Alto, CA) and TV talk show host (Tri-City Features, Fremont, CA). Many accolades later, she has founded and hosts "the SOPHIA PROJECT" - a cutting edge writing salon that weaves writing-for-performance and art-without-judgment into core community building tools.

Passion for the rhythm and music of words led DesBoine to find the advantages of independent publishing a perfect vehicle in support of the fast pace of full time writing.

The writer works her craft in California and Texas.

NOTES

Printed in Great Britain
by Amazon